ACTS OF CONTRITION

S.L. Sinclair

This book is a work of fiction. Names, items, characters, places and incidents are products of the author's imagination or are used fictitiously. Any resemblance to actual events or locales or persons, living or dead, is entirely coincidental.

Cover design by Artscandare Book Cover Design

Formatting by:

Partners in Crime Book Services

Copyright © 2024 S.L. Sinclair

All rights reserved.

No part of this book may be reproduced

or transmitted in any form or by

any means without written permission

of the author.

ISBN: 979-8-9988203-3-5

TABLE OF CONTENTS

CONTENT WARNING

<u>Please skip this next page</u>

<u>if you do not want a</u>

<u>warning.</u>

This book is, in a phrase, fucked up. It contains: noncon, dubcon, kidnapping, various forms of torture, molestation, child sex trafficking, forced prostitution, religious trauma, and more.

Please take extreme caution and understand, if you choose to NOT read this page, or choose to read further despite trepidation, that's on you, not me.

To those of you who read all this and went, "Hell yeah!", you are my people.

ALSO BY S.L. SINCLAIR

Wife for Hire

Beyond Her Duties

The Family Firm

The Family Secret

The Family Fortune

Call Me Danger

Don't Get Me Twisted

Perfect Martinis

Unbiased

Acts of Contrition

Her Secret Master

Perfect Disaster

The Vampire Mistress

Lie To Me

PLAYLIST

"The Shoulder Devil" by Dynazty

"King of Kings" by New Horizon

"In the Arms of a Devil" by Dynazty

"Deeper and Deeper" by Dave Gahan

"Instinct" by Dynazty

"Daddy" by KoRn

"Closer" by Nine Inch Nails

"Heaven's a Lie" by Lacuna Coil

"Sweet Sacrifice" by Evanescence

"All the Devils Are Here" by Dynazty

"Shot Glass of Tears" by Jung Kook

"Archangel" by Amaranthe

(Scan to play the playlist on Spotify!)

Every saint has a past.

Every sinner has a future.

~ Oscar Wilde

CHAPTER ONE

Diana

I SMELLED SHIT. As soon as I got in from school. Was the toilet overflowing?

Dad was supposed to be home, and I called for him, not wanting to go check personally. No twelve-year-old girl wants to do that, and I was no exception. I sighed, wondering if he got called in to work. He was a mechanic, and his shop was always short-handed.

I shucked my shoes in the hall closet and headed into the apartment.

Dad's silhouette was slumped in his chair, his back to me, asleep.

I assumed.

The smell was stronger now, and seemed to be coming from … him?

"Dad?" I held my breath as I crept closer, and there was something deep down inside me that felt wrong. *You should go get a neighbor*, that little voice in my head told me.

Why didn't I listen?

Better yet, why didn't I run away so I could stop everything that was going to happen to me?

Because clairvoyance isn't real. The supernatural and magic are fairy tales silly children who have never suffered believe in. I learned that the hard way.

And it all began as I stared at my father's half-open, unstaring eyes, open mouth, shit and piss-stained pants, and hands… Why do I remember the hands the most?

The blood already began to pool there, turning the fingers purple.

My dad died at thirty-eight from a heart attack.

And nothing was going to be the same.

"What will we do?" my mother

wails, looking over the due bills and

loans my dad somehow took out

without her knowing.

How was he a hundred and

seventy thousand dollars in debt? And

that isn't counting mounting interest.

What was he doing? My bet is on

gambling, but nothing in his email or

other personal effects has given Mom or

I a hint. Thank God we don't have a

house and we rent. That thing would be foreclosed on in a second.

"I could get a job," I offer tentatively. "Babysitting. Tutoring. Is a paper route still a thing?" I hate kids and teaching and don't know how to ride a bike, so none of those are exactly good options, but what can I do? We are, as Dad would have said, up Shit Creek and our paddles are broken.

Mom shakes her head. "I will figure it out. I have to."

Will you figure it out before we are homeless? I wonder, knowing our landlord won't continue being understanding due to grief. He's nice, but he's a businessman. And we need to pay rent. It's been five months and we are barely making all the bills, and rent has been late for two of those six months now.

At school, it is the only place I can escape these worries and my grief, throwing myself into classwork. I love school and learning. You could say I'm a nerd. But since I passed tests to get a scholarship to private school where at least half the students are expected to graduate and become doctors and lawyers, I'm not as bullied as I would be if I was in public school.

Principal Faulkner stops me one day on my way to class. "Miss Hill, how are you doing?"

I shrug and adjust my backpack. I haven't had a chance to put it away yet.

"Just … getting by. I've seen the school counselor as you suggested, sir."

He nods. "Good, good. You know if you ever need a non-biased, non-medical ear, my door is always open."

I try to smile but I don't think my face changes. "Thank you, sir. I will take you up on that one day." *Like Hell*, I think as I wave goodbye. I barely tell the counselor the truth, why would I tell the principal? One hint of the financial trouble we are in, and someone is sure to call CPS on my mom. No way will I let that happen.

I should add, Mom has a job. She's a cook at a local mom and pop diner, and she's good at it. But the economy sucks, she gets no tips, and hours have been cut twice in the past year and a half. It's not her fault, and I know she's been trying to find another or a second job ever since the first hour cut.

I'm a kid. I shouldn't know this. Just like I shouldn't know how to use a textbook to stop a bullet from a school shooter. But that's what the world has come to so I have to try and be practical and just support my mom.

Once I am home from school, I go to the living room and Mom has a weird look on her face.

"What happened?" I ask immediately.

"I got a second job," she says, not sounding as excited as I would assume she'd be.

"That's great! Where?" I ask, giving her a hug she only half-heartedly returns. I have a bad feeling about this job, but I know better than to tell her not to take it.

"There's a man who comes into the restaurant; he needs an after-hours assistant. You know, paperwork and things he doesn't want to leave for the next day but the nine-to-fivers won't stay overtime to do," she explains.

And she's lying. I know she's lying. I can't say how, but I know.

"Well, I guess I am old enough to stay home alone in the evenings," I say.

"It's not five nights, just three, but it will put us ahead," Mom says, and then she smiles, though it doesn't reach her eyes.

"Thank you for working hard," I tell her. "And I will do anything you need to help. All the chores, whatever."

Mom looks at me with weary eyes. "I know. That's what I hate; you need to focus on being a child as long as you can. It goes away too quickly."

How do I tell her the child she knew died the day she found her father's stinky, soiled, rigor mortis-still corpse?

CHAPTER TWO

Diana

MOM WILL WORK Wednesday, Friday, and Saturday nights. That may change as workflow changes, or so she tells me. I don't know; I've never been in an office or know what this guy does to figure out what changes would even happen.

Her first night of work is this week, and she looks much better going to this job than to cook, in a flared skirt and silk blouse with makeup on. Her leg taps the table leg as I eat dinner, and I note that she doesn't eat much.

"Mom," I say, startling her.

"Dammit."

"Sorry. I just wanna say you don't need to be worried. You'll do great."

She manages a smile. "Thank you, honey. And thank you for being able to take care of yourself. I know I won't come home to the place burnt down or worse."

I smile back. "You can trust me!" And she can. I'd rather do my homework and get in bed and read than anything else.

She gets up and kisses the top of my head. "Be good. See you in the morning."

I don't see Mom in the morning; she's still asleep when I'm ready for school. So I just leave her a note and head in. I'm sure she worked hard, right? She deserves rest.

It's when she comes home from the job at the diner I panic: she looks like death warmed over with thick, dark circles under her eyes.

"What's wrong?" I ask, hugging her tight.

She hugs me back, but weak. "I'm just not used to this, honey. It's okay. Give me time to adjust."

And she seems to adjust. Sort of. She still looks awful but as time goes by, she's functional. The bills are paid. She's back to making jokes again. In my childish mind, I fully believe we are going to be okay.

One day when I am getting in from school, I find mom frantically cleaning.

"Um, what's up?" I ask, putting my backpack on the kitchen chair.

"Mike wants to come for dinner!"

"Mike, your new boss Mike?"

"Yes, now help me once you get out of your uniform," she says.

Mom even makes me dress well, in one of my dresses I usually wear to Mass on Sundays.

"He's never met you; only seen you when you study at the counter at the diner sometimes," she explains. "So look sharp, please, sweetheart."

I do as she asks, knowing my first impression on her boss has to be important. I want Mom proud of me, and I want him to like me and approve.

When the doorbell rings, Mom rushes to get it, smoothing her skirt and fixing her hair. Sometimes, I wonder if she has a crush on him. But when he walks in the door, I have to be wrong, because he's not… Well, he's butt-ugly if I am being honest. His eyes are nice, a light shade of blue, but his beard and clothes are unkempt, and his thinning hair could use a comb or something.

He doesn't look like a wealthy businessman, but I know he is. And I know he is doing Mom a favor, so I have to be on my best behavior.

Mom taught me how to be a good hostess already; her family was old-fashioned Sicilian, so a lot of things I learned, my classmates think are stupid. It seems to make a good impression on Mike — he insists I call him that, not "Mr. Sullivan".

During dessert, he turns to Mom and says, "I was right, she is a lovely little girl, Maria."

Mom smiles. "Thank you."

"One day she could come work for me, too. She's so polite and demure, clients would love her."

There's a beat of silence, thick with tension, before I pipe up, "Maybe for an afterschool job one day. I want to work in publishing!"

Relief is palpable on Mom's face until Mike says, "A pretty thing like you wasted behind a desk? That would be a shame indeed."

I don't know why Mom wouldn't want me working for the same man she is, but she doesn't need to worry. I have my life planned out already. And I will be successful.

"Mike wants to move in," Mom tells me, nearly a year after she has been working for him. I had assumed they were dating, but I wasn't sure. Mom doesn't tell me things she deems adult business; the only reason I knew about Dad's outrageous debt was because I was in the room when she opened the emails.

The relationship doesn't come as a surprise to me; Mike even convinced Mom to quit the diner and work exclusively for him. She's been more and more tired and agitated lately, too. Overworked. Maybe this will be a good change? He will be here with her, dates will be easier. Right?

Please let me be right.

CHAPTER THREE

Diana

I WASN'T RIGHT.

I couldn't have been more wrong if I asked a Magic 8 Ball to predict the future.

Something is WRONG with my mother ever since Mike moved in. She's spacing out, eyes dull, even her voice is listless.

In fact, the only time she has looked and sounded alert was one day when Mike was out at work and she was at home. She took me aside and said in the patented Mom Voice (you know the one), "When you hear Mike's friends come by, I need you to lock your bedroom door and go to sleep with your headphones on, okay? Do you hear me?"

I nodded then, scared at the nearly frantic look in her eyes.

What is wrong with his friends?

The feeling of wrongness, of something horrible waiting to happen, follows me every day.

A few months later, I stop putting my headphones on, curiosity getting the better of me. I hear them laughing, sometimes cursing, and moaning. I hear Mom cry. I hear Mike saying, "Told you even her sloppy cunt was a perfect fuck. Nothing better than a live-in whore."

And I don't know what to say or do. Is … is this what he has had Mom doing? Why she's looked like shit for all this time? It's not office work, he's turned my mom into a prostitute.

That night, and every night after, I cry myself to sleep, but sometimes sleep doesn't come and give me a blissful respite.

Like tonight.

There are no men over, but I can hear Mike and Mom arguing. Rather, he's yelling. She's crying and saying unintelligible things.

The slap is so loud it echoes in the night and I cringe.

"I fuckin' told you what the consequences would be if you got too fucked up for me to use you or sell you at night, didn't I?" Mike shouts.

Fucked up?

That explains the rest of what my immature mind wouldn't grasp. He got her hooked on something illegal.

Bastard. I can't do anything now, but when I grow up, even a little, I vow to make him pay.

I close my eyes and stop myself from crying now; it won't help anyone, but then my bedroom door opens.

"Mom?"

"No," Mike says, his voice low.

His friends weren't over. I didn't lock my door. I thought it was safe.

"Is she okay?" I ask.

He shuts the door behind him and locks it from the inside. "She just has to sleep it off. But, you see, there were set rules I made when I took her on. One rule being, she has to be able to service me and my clients whenever we ask. No exceptions. She knew what would happen if she broke that rule.

"Looks like drugs are now more important than her precious little girl."

He gets on the bed and I try to leap out and run, but he's fast for a fat man and I'm trapped, pinned.

My nightgown tears and I scream.

"No one is going to come help you," he says conversationally as his big, gross hands part my legs.

"Please! Don't do this to me, please!" I'm just a kid, dammit.

"Now now. If you are good and be quiet, it will all be over soon," he says. "Begging won't do you any good. No one hears. No one cares."

Still I scream as the pain is unbearable, but he's right.

No one comes to help me.

And no one ever will.

The worst part about being a loner is having no close friends. And the worst part about not trusting your teachers is being unable to confide in counselors.

I'm trapped in Hell, my mom is trapped in Hell, and I don't know what to do. If I go to the cops now, they will arrest my mom for drug use and prostitution too, not caring she was forced to do both.

Mike comes to me whenever he feels like it. Once he made Mom watch, as listless and strung out as she was, as he raped my throat for nearly an hour.

"This is your fault," he told her as I cried and gagged. "Remember that."

I want him dead. I need him dead. But I'm too small, too weak, too pathetic. All I can do is pray and suffer as time passes by as if someone slowed it down like a YouTube video.

A few days after my fifteenth birthday, that's when everything comes crashing down around me like a house of cards.

"Miss Diana Hill, please report to the principal's office," comes over the loudspeakers, earning me the required jeers from the others, as if I did something wrong.

I didn't, not that I know of anyway.

When I get there, the principal, vice principal, school counselor, and a police officer stand there, all of them somber.

"What happened?"

"Diana, you might want to sit—"

"I said what happened?" I interrupt the principal, looking at the officer instead.

He sighs, mustache jiggling in the breeze.

"Miss Hill, I am very sorry to tell you this, but your mother passed away this morning due to heart failure from

the usage of illegal substances."

CHAPTER FOUR

Diana

I DON'T KNOW what to do. There wasn't even a funeral. Mike claimed Mom didn't want one, and Mom has — had — no next of kin except me, and I'm too young to make these decisions.

So now my mother is rotting in the ground in a shitty casket and I'm … I assume I will go to, like, foster care?

I hope.

But hope, to me, really is the last evil in Pandora's box.

All I can be grateful for is that Mom isn't suffering anymore. She's free, finally. Honestly, I'm jealous.

On Monday after Mom passed, I get up and get ready for school, only for Mike to stop me at the door.

"Where do you think you're going?" he asks.

"School," I reply warily. "Like every weekday."

"Not anymore. Your legal guardian pulled you out in favor of … learning from home." That smile on his face makes me sick.

"Who?" I ask, hoping that means I'll be moving out soon.

"Me. Now, get back in that bedroom and don't come out unless I give you permission. And leave your uniform on," he commands.

My mouth drops. "No, how can you be—"

"I can be anything I want to be with the right connections, money, and favors. Now get the *fuck* in your room." He slaps me so hard my head tilts and hair flies. "I planned all this for a long fucking time, and now it's time to get the rewards of my work. You're going to make me even richer."

Planned … what? He's not saying…

I lunge at him, getting one good punch to his flabby face. "*You killed my mother!* That was no accident, you bastard!"

He laughs and catches me, carrying me like a sack of potatoes into my room. He drops me on the bed and I try to get up but he hits me in the gut so hard I lose air and fall back.

"She was of good use to me, but you? You are a fucking gold mine. But you're going to have to lose some of that fat to look younger, smaller, for longer. Maybe I can pass you off as fourteen or even thirteen."

"I will get to the cops somehow," I say. "You're not getting away with this!"

"Do you think even if I let you out, you'd escape me? The police are in my pocket, you stupid cunt." He smiles and shuts the door. I hear a lock turning, sealing me in with my fate.

I sob for a while, anger and grief and fear taking over my mind.

Sometime in the afternoon, I hear the lock on the door jingle.

"Get up, bitch," Mike says. "Your first client is here, and he's waited a long, long time to have a piece of you."

He leaves and his bulk is replaced with a familiar face.

Principal Faulkner.

I knew he was a creep! I knew it! I made sure I was never alone with him because he weirded me out so much.

"Now that your generous guardian has you out of school and

living up to your full potential, I felt it was only right I be the first to break you in," he says, closing the door behind him.

"Fuck you," I snap.

He clucks his tongue. "Looks like I need to shut that smart mouth up." He grabs me by the hair with one hand and undoes his pants with the other, bringing out his old, wrinkly, hard cock.

When he shoves it into my mouth, I act on instinct and bite down so hard, hot, coppery blood squirts out, hitting the roof of my mouth. He screams, and the sound is music to my ears.

I gnaw on it, feeling flesh tear beneath my teeth, my mouth filling with more blood. My heartbeat races and I feel alive. For the first time in three years, I feel powerful and … happy.

I'm happy as I bite his dick off, listening to my abuser scream.

He hits me in the jaw and I release his cock, spitting out blood as I do so, and smile at him. Can he see his blood and flesh in my teeth? I hope so.

His miserable cock is disfigured, some of it hanging off, and he lunges for me, but adrenaline and instinct guide me and I attack first, raking my nails down his winkled cheeks. One nail snags his lower eyelid and tears, making him cry tears of blood. The other leaves deep gouges in his cheek.

Faulkner screams louder, angrier, and filled with pain.

The fire in my veins is reaching fever pitch. A few minutes more, and I think I could kill him with my bare hands, and I am *dying* to find out if I can.

The door opens then, and I sadly can't fight off two men as Mike comes in and shouts something I can't even decipher.

They both lift me and as they begin to beat me, hitting every available surface, including my face, I still smile that bloody smile.

I tasted joy for a fleeting moment. That has to be enough.

When I come to again, my first

thought is, if I keep passing out like

that, I am going to get brain damage.

My second is, where the Hell am I?

The room is all white with bright

fluorescent lights and I smell antiseptic.

Did I need to go to the hospital?

"She's coming to, Doctor," a

woman says, voice dispassionate.

"Oh, too bad she didn't wake

when I was using her tight cunt," a man

replies. "She's numbed, she can stay

awake for the rest of this. I'm almost done with the hysterectomy."

The *what*?

My head is spinning and I can't wrap it around what he just said. Isn't that for women in menopause and, God forbid, cancer?

"Welcome back, whore," Mike says from a chair across the room. It takes all my energy to look at him. "While you passed out, I figured it was time to get you here and get you fixed up to be my perfect sex slave. After all, we can't have babies getting in the way. Too many variables, though selling it would make me a pretty penny. I need to be smart, not greedy. Your holes for the next few years are good enough, and

39

most men don't want to wear a condom. They want to think they're breeding a little teenage cow like you."

He walks over and grabs my breasts, which I now see are in a hospital gown. "You'll be ready to go in a month for full-body. They can use your mouth and your udders for now. Doctor Kelvin here had the pleasure of being the last man to cum in your fertile womb before he removed it himself.

"Poetic, isn't it?"

I don't answer.

I can't.

The power and jubilation I felt earlier are gone now, replaced by a dark despondency I fear will never leave me.

I had a momentary victory.

He won the war.

This act, this destruction of my future, is finally what breaks me.

CHAPTER FIVE

Diana

IT IS EASY to keep track of days; I can still see the light through the boards on the window. I know it will be nearly three years soon since I have been held captive, since my mother died, since my life became whittled down to this quagmire of pain and depravity.

Since I became a child sex slave.

You hear about these sorts of horror stories on the internet, or in movies. You never think you will be in one, and have the starring role no less.

I stopped begging God to kill me. Either He isn't real or He has no intention of allowing my suffering to cease. Even if I went to Hell, no way would it be half as vicious as my living reality.

I just want it all to stop.

As I muse, the door opens. I don't flinch anymore. Let whatever may come just kill me quicker.

Mike tosses an apple and a bottle of water at me; both fall to the floor by the bed. "Finish those and wash your fucking stench. Tonight's going to be a big one."

I don't respond, and usually he doesn't care. Today, it's different.

"Don't you want to know why, cunt?"

I don't even dignify him with a shake of my head.

"Tomorrow's your birthday. You're gonna be an adult. And that means most of the clients who pay for you won't anymore. They don't have any interest in grown ass women."

That makes me start, and he chuckles at the reaction. It's my birthday? I note the passage of time, not the dates.

"So get ready. Tonight is the last hurrah." With that, he leaves.

What does he mean by a last hurrah?

Is he finally going to fucking end my miserable existence? Or will he just find new clients who don't mind someone over eighteen?

Will I ever be free?

I can barely hear Mike on the phone all afternoon, talking to a lot of people.

What if he sells me? He's done that, he told me. But this new person could be worse. But I could also escape easier.

Worrying about it won't help. Just deal with it as it comes, my conscience scolds.

Later that night, I hear voices. A lot of voices. All men from the sound of it, though I know it's not unusual for a woman or two to come see me. But … that's a lot of people.

I feel dread settle into my stomach, my nervous system recognizing the danger before my brain will ever acknowledge it. The less I address it, the less it can traumatize me.

The door to my bedroom opens, and Mike stands there, a clear path outside right in front of me, but I am far too cowed to take it.

"Come on, bitch," he practically barks. "This room is too small. Get out there."

Is this a trick? No, it can't be.

There are people out in the living room,

after all. Tentatively, I stand, holding

my breath as I walk past him. I expect

him to grab me by the hair and beat me

for daring to leave the bedroom, but he

doesn't. He shuts that door and follows

me into the living room where ten …

eleven … twelve men stand around.

Some have bottles of beer like this is a

party.

"All right!" Mike calls from

behind me, voice loud above the din,

and I flinch. "It is eight in the evening.

We have until midnight for her to still

be to your specific tastes. All former

rules I had in place are out the window.

Do what you want, how you want,

where you want with this cunt. You paid well to let your darkest selves out; get your money's worth."

He shoves me forward into the waiting arms of the first man. I think I recognize him; I think I recognize a few of them. Honestly, it's been a blur and my brain has rejected or compartmentalized most of it.

The man grins wickedly and the next thing I know, my cheek stings and my head whips so fast, I may have whiplash from his punch.

The music turns up, a severely loud bass that is likely to cover up any sounds that get made. The neighbors won't call the cops for a party with music, but they might for a gangrape.

Might.

The man tosses me onto the floor
and more hands grab at me, holding me
aloft, legs spread, as a cock pierces my
unprepared pussy. That's the only time
I usually scream, the pain is too bad
with that first thrust before my body
adjusts and tears come to my eyes
quickly.

Tonight, I think that will be the
least of my pain.

I can't fully detail it all; all I can
recall is fiery pain, cocks over and over
in every hole. They force me to vomit
and then go back to throatfucking me,
calling me a fat pig, a whore, disgusting,
not even worthy of their cum.

When the first cock penetrates my ass, I feel something tear and start to cry. Blood drips down my thighs but they don't care, they laugh as they trade off between them, sometimes two cocks at once.

I want to die.

And then the beatings start. My ribs take the worst of it, and something snaps, sharp pain making me gasp as I lose air for a moment.

My nose shatters from a boot to the face, and things start to get hazy.

Laughter can barely be heard above the loud bass bumping from the speakers, but I can see the crazed joy on their faces, and it hits me.

I really am going to die.

None of these men would care if I died now; they'd keep fucking my body as long as it was still warm and pliant.

Four hours must pass, but I spend the last of it in a haze of pain. Nose, ribs, I think maybe my cheekbone: all broken. Asshole torn and bleeding. Maybe my pussy too, I don't know.

The last thing I remember hearing is Mike saying, "Time's almost up, finish up and we can dump the body."

The darkness is fading. There's a hazy gray light, and I feel like I'm floating.

"Mom? Dad?"

"Honey, don't try to move or talk too soon." It's a woman's voice, low with a soothing but stern tone.

My eyes open more, and I'm not dead. I'm in … an infirmary? The light hurts my head; my whole body aches somewhere beneath the floaty feeling.

Turning my head, I see a beautiful woman, maybe in her mid-twenties, with long black hair and equally dark eyes.

"Where… Who…"

She shushes me sharply this time, not mean but more like a sister.

"My name's Vera. I run this blood bank. I happened to be taking a walk last night and found you. Do you remember anything?" the woman asks tentatively.

I do. Of course I do.

"Please…" My voice is raw from screaming last night. "He can't find me. He thinks I'm dead. If I'm alive he'll finish the job."

Vera nods as if she understands. "You're not the first woman I've found like this. I am sure you sadly won't be the last. But rest now. Your nose wasn't broken, but you're pretty bruised in the face. Your ribs will take time to finish setting, but we managed to snap them back into place.

"When you wake up, we will plan the rest of your life, your freedom."

It turns out Vera is just basically a good Samaritan who has helped people for all reasons. I don't really know. Once she took me to a women's shelter and the older lady there praised her, she vanished. I had so many questions, but no way to reach her.

"She's like Batman," the woman, Hattie, comments. "Saves men, women, children, animals, and then vanishes into the night as if she was never here."

"She shouldn't have saved me," I admit quietly.

"Why not, honey?"

"I can't survive this world. I'm too broken. I've been too broken for a long time."

Hattie kneels down so she's at eye-level with me. "Broken things can be fixed. We will fill those cracks with gold."

I don't think it's gold, per se, but the shelter sets me up with a counselor who, after realizing I will not speak of anything in detail, switches her focus to me being well enough to live on my own, to not succumb to flashbacks.

Other women at the shelter teach me basic cooking skills, and how to work most appliances. Mom had taught me, but things have changed since she did so on our old, outdated things.

"Why the Hell does a fridge need to talk?" I ask, and the other women find me hilarious.

"Better than a man talking," one of them comments, and the others all agree.

What if they knew women hurt me too? That it's not just men who do unspeakable acts?

My ribs heal. My mind doesn't, but my soul begins to do … something. Call it hardening.

Mike wanted me dead. He expected me to have no life after he took away my childhood. For the first time since I was thirteen, I didn't do what he wanted.

I survived.

I wanted to die, but I didn't.

So now I have to live, if only to spite him.

The shelter has a network of apartments who will rent via cash payment and to women who have no credit and are looking to hide from abusers or have fallen on hard times. This landlord is new to the network and he doesn't question me when I say I don't even have a job yet.

"Rent is due on the first. You get three days' grace period," Rick tells me. "I'm sure it will all work out."

I spent three months at the shelter, and now I have my own place. It's tiny, and dingy, but it's mine. Mine to decorate, mine to live in, mine to be safe in.

When the women see the movers out — all furniture is donated secondhand, but I don't mind — I burst into relieved tears.

Is this my life? Really? Truly?

Did I go from three years of total horror, preceded by two years of abuse, to actual freedom?

It seems too good to be true.

Of course, things that seem too good to be true often are.

I cannot find a job. At all. Not a single place has hired me or called me back. Some wanted me to be bilingual, others didn't trust that I don't know my own social security number. And the list goes on.

The night before the first of the month hits, I make a decision after over

a week of intense internal deliberation
with my conscience.

I have to use what I have to make
money. The one thing I'm good at. The
only thing I'm good at.

The realization I have to be my
own pimp, sell myself to earn my
freedom, causes me to break down once
more in tears. I cry for so long I pass
out, salt tracks drying on my face.

Reality fucking sucks, and
freedom is an illusion. We are all bound
to something, usually money and debt.
For some it's a soul-sucking desk job.
For others like me, it's selling away my
very soul along with my body.

I apparently was so exhausted I
don't hear anyone enter my apartment.

I'm blissfully ignorant until a weight settles on my mattress and my eyes open automatically, thinking it's Mike.

And honestly, what is the difference that it's not?

Rick kneels over me, his cock out of his pants, rage in his eyes. The same sort of anger and insanity I saw in every man Mike sent to hurt me.

"No." It's not a plea. It's a command. "You're supposed to be here for women who need help!"

He slaps me. "Dumb whore. I let cunts like you in because it's so easy to fuck your lying, lazy, sloppy pussies and who are you going to report me to? You're no one. Nothing. You have nothing. They'd laugh you out of the police station but probably not before using you too."

He paws at my oversized shirt and it tears at the collar. He's like an animal as he forces me down, forces my legs open. "This is what happens to whores who don't pay their rent on the first. You get three days of this until it's paid.

"After that, you're my property to sell."

CHAPTER SIX

Diana

I NEVER REALLY fully understood the meaning of the word irony until now.

I escaped my captor who forced me to have sex against my will only to move into a place where the landlord also forced me, and in order to get that to stop I have to … have sex for money by my will.

Irony at its finest.

I'm trying to not fall back into flashbacks, trying to remind myself I am choosing this. This is a choice, because I have no work experience and no luck landing literally any job. Even a cashier position, picking up trash, anything. I don't know, maybe it's that I don't know how to write a resume, let alone that I don't have one to write anyway.

But this is the life I was thrown into. And dammit, I want to survive!

And I can control what happens to me. I set the rules, I decide who has access to me. I decide how much I am worth.

That makes me feel better. Stronger. And as the time has gone by, I can slowly buy new furniture. A small

TV. Softer mattress. Better food, though I still struggle with eating and looking and feeling too fat to be desired.

These men I attract on the street, though, they don't seem to be looking for someone who looks young. They want an adult. That's a first for me, and strangely, it's also a confidence-booster.

This night on the street, the girl I usually stand near sighs. Her name on the street is Sin. No clue what her real name is, nor do I care. As long as she stands near me, I always wind up getting the first pick of men.

"What's your problem?" I ask.

"Look." She discreetly points to three people.

A beautiful woman maybe a decade or more older than me in a white silk coat and pumps, a bearded man in his late thirties also in white, and a third man, maybe thirty, with long blond hair in a low ponytail, wearing dark slacks and a white dress shirt. They are too well-dressed to be around here unless they're looking to rent one of us for the night. I will stay far away from that — I refuse to entertain groups.

"Who are they?" I ask.

"They're from the First Church of the New Disciples," she whispers. "A religious group. They are always trying to save our souls. I keep hoping Blondie over there will come around, literally, but it's like they're made of stone," Sin complains.

I can see why she wants him to come around in all forms of the word. He's handsome. But a pretty face does nothing for me. Nor do any of these men I have been with. Pretty sure any potential sex drive I could have had has been eradicated from within me thanks to Mike and his clients.

The woman and bearded man stay together, while the blond man walks towards Sin and I. She clearly gets ready to present, but I can tell when someone won't be interested in what we're offering.

Well … maybe he would be if he was alone. Not with his fellowship members.

"Sin," he greets the girl at my side. "Even a few church visits couldn't manage to at least make you think twice about coming back here?"

She giggles and I want to slap her or myself, or him for entertaining her.

He turns away from her, eyes on me. I won't lie, his gaze is unnerving. It feels like he sees past this exterior and can read my very soul. Like he can see my pain, my sins, and my indifference to it all.

"I haven't seen you around; it saddens me that this profession is gaining members rather than losing."

He sighs. "My name is Brother Thomas, I'm a Pastor-in-Training with the First Church of the New Disciples. And you do not have to do this, Miss…"

"Lily."

"Lily." He smiles as he repeats my fake name. "Tell me, why do this? Why give away the precious body God gave you?"

"I'm not giving it, I'm selling it. No one gets me for free," I reply curtly. "And if you don't mind, Pastor—"

"In-Training," he interrupts. "Not a pastor yet."

"Well, good for you. If you don't mind, men won't approach me if you're talking to me."

He gives me a smile that I am sure has made women become putty in his hands. Too bad I'm immune to charm.

"You're destroying your precious soul," he comments, handing me a tract.

I wave it away. "Pastor, my soul was destroyed a long time ago and I had nothing to do with it."

Thomas

Earlier that day…

"Brother Thomas," Father Oliver calls as he sees me coming back from one of my regular nature walks. They're to keep fit, keep active, not go stir-crazy, and get inspiration for my sermons. I take them regularly enough, most of our community knows to find me near the wooded area as opposed to my house.

"Father," I greet him politely. "What has sent you here this afternoon?" Being albino, he usually avoids the daylight.

"I would like you to take over for me tonight, ministering to the lost in the city," he says. Falling into step with me, we head back to the residential section of our compound.

"Am I ready for that, do you think? To lead the others alone?"

"You've been Pastor-in-Training for six months; I believe you were ready when you began," Oliver admits. "God is telling me you are needed there more than I am."

Unlike a lot of pastors who start these sort of communities, God doesn't speak to Father Oliver that much. When He does, it is usually something monumental, like when Oliver started the community, rescued his wife Catherine, and set the rules for us who choose to surrender ourselves to God and forsake the outside world and its growing evils. God tells him who to choose to study under him — me — and how to properly indoctrinate rescued spouses. Also what punishments fit each broken rule a community member makes, and who can mete out said punishments.

So if Father Oliver says God is telling him I need to go minister to the heathens, who am I to argue?

I admit I am good at public speaking, and I can be convincing. In my former life, I could have people eating out of the palm of my hand right before I ended their miserable lives, and they'd thank me for the privilege.

Of course, that life and all its perks are behind me for the most part.

However, I retained my deliberate charm, which makes me an excellent Pastor-in-Training.

I choose my fellow church members, Brother Joseph and Sister Lisa, and we leave for the city after dinner, when the freaks truly do come out.

Since one prostitute for some reason seemed to take too much of a liking to me, I usually stick to the homeless and the youth who could easily have been me when I was their age. Before I surrendered my sin to the church, I was as wanton as these women; who am I to tell them to stop? And how much temptation can I take before I take one and kill them, going

back to all my former sin and erasing
my progress?

But this is God's will, not mine.
And so we go, tracts in hand, God at our
backs.

By the way, if an attractive
person tells you they don't know they're
good looking, they're lying. We all
know, and we all use it to our
advantage. Especially somewhere like
this, where my appearance gets me all
the attention I could want. I never paid
for a woman, though, and even if I
wasn't in the church, I would not start
now.

I could get these sluts to let me
sleep with them and kill them if I

wanted with just a few words and a smile.

"Lisa, cinch your jacket a bit more before some passing creep thinks you're one of the whores," I scold my older sister when she gets out of the car.

She rolls her eyes at me but does as I say, and of course she begins to tease me. Being my actual sibling, she gets a pass at what would usually not be allowed.

I am not listening. I can't listen. My attention has been completely arrested as my eyes land on the most beautiful young woman I have ever seen.

A few things about her stand out: her thinness, as if she is overcoming a long illness, the fact that her slim body does not diminish the round swell of her breasts in her corset top, and her eyes. Her eyes are wide and deep brown, expressive and bright. These are not the eyes of a whore, a sex worker. No. They are innocent.

That is what strikes me most of all, this air of quietness, of almost childlike wonder.

My heart and soul have wholly been possessed in this moment, and I forget where I am and why I came.

"Little brother dear." Lisa snaps her fingers to get my attention. "What happened?"

I shake my head, unable to speak of it now. "Nothing. Let's begin."

I walk purposefully to this sweet

little sinner I spotted, knowing one

thing as a sure fact. This woman came

from God, just as He speaks to Father

Oliver. He sent her to me, or rather, He

sent me to her.

This girl belongs to me, and I will

save her.

CHAPTER SEVEN

Diana

Two weeks later…

IT FEELS NICE to have extra cash and pay rent early so I can take this weekend off and catch up on things I like, things I didn't have a chance to while Mike held me captive.

Today, I'm watching the official uploads from a music festival overseas. I had no idea until today that the bands I liked when I was fourteen are still going, and I settle in with a blanket and a cup of coffee, ready to relax. Maybe feel like a normal almost-nineteen-year-old for once.

Until a door slams across the hall, so hard the building shakes. I close my eyes, sighing. Was it Mrs. Thompson or the other guy I haven't officially met?

When a tentative but frantic knock comes at my apartment door, I get my answer. When I open the door, Mrs. Thompson has a vicious bruise across her eye and cheek. She's holding an ice pack to it.

"Fucking Rick?" I guess, letting her inside.

"I let him know in advance I'd be two hundred short on rent and have it by the third and he decided to let me know how much he appreciated my heads up." Her voice trembles even as she sounds angry. "But that's not the worst part."

It doesn't look like he assaulted her, not going by her clothes and face, so what's worse?

"He's coming back this afternoon. When Whitney gets home from school."

My whole body freezes at that implication. "You're fucking with me."

She shakes her head and bursts into tears. She's much older than me, but she's so small, so frail, so sweet.

Things I never got to be. Learning the hard way what the world is like to women at thirty-something? That has to be a shock.

"Let me hide her tonight. He can't stay at your place forever," I suggest. "I'd say I'd hide you, too, but he obviously knows where you live and will come back. But at least this way…"

This is bullshit. I have to tell a woman she's going to be assaulted just to protect someone even more vulnerable.

Mrs. T keeps nodding as she tries to catch her breath. "Yes, please. I will deal with whatever he does to me, just please protect her."

So, that afternoon, Mrs. T ushers little Whitney over to my place.

"But I don't understand," the kid says once her mom kisses her goodbye. She puts her backpack on my threadbare secondhand couch. "What does Mom need to do?"

"Just a grown-ups' meeting," I tell her. "Want a snack?" I don't have much, I still don't eat much, but I have chocolate pudding pops and Whitney happily eats one.

"Hey, I have something I need to read, but do you want to watch TV? You can put it as loud as you want," I tell her. "In fact, blast it so I can hear it out here, okay? The TV is in my room."

Her big eyes light up and she gives me a slightly sticky hug. "You are so cool for an adult!"

She literally dashes away and just in time, as I hear Rick calling for Mrs. Thompson, banging on her door.

Whitney has found the YouTube app on my crappy smartTV and the sounds of a popular song about love seven days a week should be enough to drown out the sounds I can barely hear out here.

Closing my eyes, I try to stave off flashbacks.

You're out of there now, my conscience reminds me. *And you're helping another child not be in your position.*

I can't believe the neighbors don't report the sounds coming from the Thompsons' apartment, but maybe they're used to it. Maybe they were threatened too. Maybe the men wish it was them doing it. Who knows?

It feels like hours before the sounds stop and I hear Rick shout, "If that two hundred isn't there by tomorrow this time, there's nowhere you or your fucking slut daughter can hide from me. You will get that money, or she'll earn it."

No. Fuck no, Hell no, just *no*.

I'd rather die than know a child will go through what I did.

There goes my weekend off. But it will be worth it.

After I ensure Mrs. Thompson is okay and help her in the aftermath, I send Whitney home and get ready to go to my usual spot in the city.

I sigh to myself, wishing I didn't have such a big heart. But if Mrs. Thompson doesn't have that last $200, I don't think I can hide her daughter any longer than I did today. And then what happens to Whitney? She's fucking twelve, she doesn't deserve this, any of this.

Just like I didn't.

One more sigh and I round the corner where some of the other girls stand and assess them.

Stand near the uglier ones, or the ones whose bodies don't look as good.

That's how you get chosen. Sad but true;
I guess I got blessed with being pretty so
I could have some sort of living … even
if I'd rather die.

And if I wasn't worried about
Whitney and her mom, I'd do it. No one
would look for me until long after I was
dead and my rent was late. Or they
smelled my rotting corpse. Whichever.

*Okay, Diana. Stop thinking and go
out there and present,* I scold myself and
step forward. I see Sin turn to look at me
and grimace. I usually stand near her.
Her pink hair gets attention, and then
they spot me and choose me over her
nearly emaciated form. Despite the fact
I'm still extremely thin, my boobs
always get attention.

I don't stand near her tonight.

Look at me, being so altruistic.

After fifteen minutes, I check my crappy watch and wonder if I would be better off going to one of the hidden brothels. I don't like to share my earnings, but it would be faster.

And then a familiar white BMW pulls up, automatic windows rolling down to reveal the man behind the wheel. The handsome one who keeps trying to "save" us working girls. He has shown up four times in the past two weeks. If he starts his spiel tonight, I am gonna knee him in the balls. He's alone though. Usually he's with one or two others when he heads down here.

"Lily." Hearing my street name from his lips surprises me. Green eyes pierce me even from a couple yards away. If I was a respectable young woman, I'd have considered dating him. But men like him won't sully themselves with my ilk. No, they have their Stepford Wives-in-waiting.

Girls like me are the ones they fuck behind the wives' backs.

I step forward, leaning into the window out of habit. He doesn't even glance at my tits, just like last time, and this time they're literally right in his face.

"How can I help you, Pastor?" I ask.

"In-training," he corrects with a charming smile, like every time. The locks click open. "You can get in."

I resist the urge to smirk at him. I knew he was just another red-blooded perverted man, religion be damned. I should have made a bet with the others. Oh well, at least now I get to brag about being right.

Opening the door, I slide in, feeling the heated seat below me, the leather soft as butter. Christian rock plays on the radio, and it smells like aftershave, but not overpowering. Indeed, his blond goatee looks neatly and newly trimmed. He drives about half a mile before turning into an abandoned alley. Unbuckling his seatbelt, he turns to face me.

"You realize you don't get free favors just because you're a man of God," I quip.

He nods. "Nothing free is worth having, Diana."

I go to reply when my body seizes up, hearing a name he never should have known. No one knew it aside from Rick and those who bothered to check my name on my mailbox in the building.

"What did you call me?" I ask, trying to keep my voice level.

"The name your mother gave you, baptized you with," he replies, his voice still soft and even.

"How do you know that?"

"Oh, sweet, sinful girl, I know everything about you. And I'm going to save you."

He reaches across me to the glove compartment and I barely move, too shocked. When he pulls out a hypodermic needle, I rush to unbuckle my seatbelt, but he's too fast; he's done this before or practiced to get every movement precise.

The needle pierces my neck and he depresses the plunger even as I try to fight him off. For being a slim man, he certainly is strong.

The drug must be a sedative, and injected in my carotid, it begins to hit me in maybe two minutes, as I feel my strength flagging and my head growing woozy.

He gently pries me off him and fixes my seatbelt. "We don't want you getting hurt if I make a sudden stop."

"I'll … fuckin' kill you," I rasp out, eyes drooping.

He looks at me and smiles. "Sleep, Diana."

And I do.

CHAPTER EIGHT

Diana

MY ASSHOLE GUARDIAN did a lot of shit to me, but he never drugged me. In fact, I never even smoked pot, let alone took "downers". My mouth is like a desert, and my eyes take forever to properly open. Even as I open them, the meager light shining in here hurts so bad, I squeeze them shut again. I'm pretty sure my head weighs more than the rest of my body.

Okay, Di. You need to figure out where you are, and to do that, you need to sit up and open your eyes.

I decide maybe sitting up with my eyes closed is the best option, so I do, feeling something thin under me, like a cot cushion. I scoot myself back, hitting something metal.

I was right, though. Sitting up, then opening my eyes quells some of the dizziness I feel. It's what I see that I'm not prepared for.

I'm in some sort of basement or dungeon. The walls are stone, the floor concrete. There's a single window set high against the ceiling, too small for a grown human to crawl out of it. It looks sealed, but I can't be sure.

The room is barren, the light coming from a bare bulb set in the center of the ceiling. There's a switch for it near a door I am positive is locked. Another open, smaller door reveals a bathroom that wouldn't look out of place in a prison cell, but the light in there is off, so I can only make out a toilet, sink, and old-fashioned bathtub and shower head.

I am on a bed, it seems. This, too, wouldn't be out of place in prison. The thin, white mattress is covered with a white sheet, and there's a flat white pillow. The bed frame is metal, also white, with bars at the head and foot.

"What the fuck?" I mutter when I look down at myself and don't see my black pleated miniskirt and red top, but instead a flowy white nightgown that reminds me a little of Carrie's prom dress, sans blood.

My bra is gone too, and my panties don't feel like the black silk ones I put on before going out. I move the sheet lightly covering my legs back and, before I can check my underwear, I realize the weight I felt on my ankle is not my high heel dangling by its strap.

One ankle is in a black cuff, chained to the bed.

It is then the panic swells in my chest, bursting forth like a racehorse.

I'm trapped.

Fucking kidnapped and chained up like a dog.

I kick the sheet the rest of the way off and stand up, wondering how much slack the chain has, its strength, and how the Hell I can get out of here.

Don't panic now, I tell myself. *You were locked up for three fucking years, you will not allow someone to do it again!* What

I need is to not be so weak and shaky from whatever he dosed me with.

If the chain is long enough, I can strangle him with it.

This basement is huge, spanning the whole length of the house above, and as soon as I test the chain, I realize no way in Hell will I reach the door. Or the lightswitch, for that matter.

He could leave me down here in the dark if he chose, for as long as he chose.

Panic swells again as I think about that and I crush it down. I go the other way, ensuring I don't move too fast and make myself trip like some bad horror movie heroine.

I can reach the bathroom, and the light in there is motion-censored, turning on when I step through the threshold. As I expected, it's dingy; clean, but old and worn. There's a bar of unopened soap, toilet paper, and a few thin towels on the counter by the sink.

It hits me that I'm barefoot, but the basement is pleasantly warm. I'm not cold even when stepping on concrete. Well, not freezing to death isn't exactly a comfort right now.

Then another thought hits me.

I keep assuming Pastor-in-Training Thomas took me.

What if he didn't? What if he sold me or something?

I feel nauseous and lean against the bathroom door frame — the bathroom itself has no door — and take deep breaths. In the thick silence, I hear boots on stairs on the other side of the door.

When it opens, I almost feel relieved when Thomas walks through the threshold.

"Good, you're awake," he says, closing the door behind him. "And … dizzy?"

I shake my head. Do I fight? I'd likely lose. But the alternative is, yet again, letting a man do whatever the fuck he wants to me. He will hurt me anyway; why shouldn't I get a few meager licks in first?

He steps closer and I decide to be stupid as Hell and lunge at him. I land a punch to his chest and he laughs.

Laughs!

Strong hands grip my shoulders and he holds me still, looking down at me with curious, calm eyes.

He doesn't *look* crazy. Mike, all the men he brought to me, they all had either a crazy or evil gleam in their eyes. Enjoyment. Thomas has none of those things.

"Little sinner, you continue to intrigue me even as you seal your fate," he says. "We have always fought against the things best for our well-being, haven't we? When as babies we fought against the doctor for vaccinations, as small children we fought against naps, against vegetables… But the doctors and our parents always won out, hm?" He runs one hand in my hair and I flinch. "I will win out against your innate sin."

Okay, I take it back. This fucker is batshit crazy for real.

"What exactly are you doing with me?" I ask.

The hand in my hair brushes along my cheek now, and I flinch again, moving away, making him grab my chin so I can't move my head.

"You were made for me," he says. "I knew the moment I saw you. That is why we kept coming around where I knew you would be working.

Trying to save you. And yet you always rebuffed me, promiscuity and lust more important than the plan God has for you."

"Made … for you," I say, trying to wrap my head around the cuckoo bullshit coming out of his mouth.

Why are the hot ones always gay or insane?

He nods, green eyes shining in the dim light. "I brought Father Oliver along with me one day, but we didn't exit the car. He observed you. And he agrees, if I feel in my soul you were made to be my wife, he wants us to be happy."

"My dude, there is no 'us'," I blurt out. "How long have you stalked me to know my real name anyway?"

"It was not *stalking*; that's such a cold word," Thomas comments. "I needed to ensure I wasn't being led astray by your appearance, and to know how deep your sin ran. I needed to be certain what I felt for you was real, my little dove, before I brought you here and began my work."

"Your work?"

"Undoing the damage sin has caused to your body and soul." He raises my face to meet his eyes, and he looks … excited? "As long as it takes, whatever it takes, I will remove the stain on your soul and make you pure, worthy of being my wife, worthy of belonging to our holy community."

It's not a church. It's a fucking cult.

I can't let him see he's making me panic. I have to let him believe he can't hurt me, whatever his plans may be.

"Yeah? You want to purify me? Then do your worst."

He grins, and that's where the crazy shows. That smile would enjoy fileting someone's skin in a dark basement … sort of like this one.

"Oh, little dove, I do love a challenge."

CHAPTER NINE

Diana

HE JUST LEAVES after that. No goodbye. No more threats. Remaining where I am, near the bathroom, I sink down to the floor, my knees shaking so bad I can't be held up any longer.

How did this happen to me?

Again?

No, not again.

Mike was cold and calculating, yes, and he planned my captivity and forced prostitution for a long time. Same as Thomas planned on kidnapping me. But the reasons are clearly different.

Will the methods be?

In the ten months since Mike set me free — if we can call it that — I may have remained a sex worker, but I had control. As long as I paid the landlord, I could control who touched me, how, when, and what I got in return. It wasn't ideal, but I was free.

Now once more a man has decided what to do with my existence, and I hate this. But this … I don't see a way out. If this is a "community", it stands to reason more cult members live nearby. Even if I could get out of this chain, someone would see me and bring me back.

I *can't* be raped again, forced. I can't go through it anymore.

Don't cry, I tell myself as tears well up in my eyes. *Don't you dare shed a single tear because of a man again.*

The door opens, and I jump, but my legs don't carry me and I flop onto my ass, hitting my back hard against the wall.

Thomas carries a tray, giving me a curious look.

"You need to eat, Diana. The sedative made you sleep through the night."

It's morning? Hell, I didn't even know. I didn't think to ask.

He places the tray on the bed and bends down by me, observing me. Studying me. He sighs. "I calculated based on your estimated weight — did you know you're severely underweight for one of your build? Anyway, it appears you are not accustomed to medications or even illegal drugs for it to have hit you this hard. That is my mistake, and I will atone for it. Here."

Before I realize what's happening, Thomas picks me up as if I really do weigh nothing and deposits me on the bed.

"Eat. I will return later. If you are still feeling severe effects such as dizziness, our community doctor will see you."

No. No. No private, community doctors. Not after my stepfather's "friend" happily removed my reproductive organs without my consent or proper knowledge.

"No," I say, hating how weak my voice sounds. "No doctor. I'll be fine."

Thomas nods, apparently seeing I'm serious. "Good. Because we have to begin your training, and I would prefer to do so immediately."

I glance at the tray; it holds a bowl of oatmeal with fruit, a cup of what looks like black tea, another of milk, 2 eggs, and some sort of meat. Maybe turkey sausage?

I don't usually eat this much, but what will happen if I don't?

I wonder briefly if he's going to drug me again, but he doesn't seem like that's on his agenda. That was only to get me here. Now that I'm here, it's clear he wants me alert for whatever he's going to do to me.

I manage to eat half the plate and finish the tea and half the milk when Thomas returns. My eyes follow him warily as he picks up the tray and glances. My body automatically tenses, sure he's going to be upset, but why would he give me so much food anyway? If what he said is true and he wants me as his crazy psycho-bride, wouldn't he be worried if I got fat? I already gained weight since I went on my own.

"Not fond of eggs?" he asks.

I shake my head.

"I expect you to speak when I am asking you a direct question, Diana." His voice is soft but stern. That's different. Mike preferred me to be silent.

"No, I just … it's been a long time since I could eat a lot. That's all."

"I see. I will lower the portions and bring you more slowly over your time here with me."

"Why?" It just slips out and I hate myself. Closing my eyes, I brace myself for a punch or a slap but it doesn't come.

"Why do I want you to *eat*?" he says slowly.

Opening my eyes, he watches me as if I am a zoo exhibit he can't wait to write up a scientific report on.

I nod. "Yes. Why?"

"You are an interesting woman, little sinner. I will return later on." He turns and leaves without another word, quietly in control of everything.

Even me.

It doesn't matter if the end result is different, a man still wants to tell me what to do and how to eat, how to live.

What did I ever do to deserve this?

A noise jolts me; apparently the remainder of the drug made me doze off. Immediately I notice my head feels better now and I am no longer dizzy as I sit up.

Thomas has entered the room, standing at the foot of the bed, watching me. I'm not used to this. Not used to being clothed in bed, not used to a man not touching me as he pleases. This is not how I would expect being kidnapped to go.

"Your eyes are clearer," he comments, his voice soft and deep. "Dizzy?"

I shake my head.

"*Speak* when spoken to," he commands.

"Not dizzy anymore, um, sir." Should I be this polite? Should I call him 'Pastor' instead? I just want this to be a nightmare, but since it's reality, I have to do what I can to make it bearable.

His lips lift in a smirk. "You don't have to call me sir, but I can admit I like the way it sounds from my fiancée."

His what now?

Crazy son of a bitch.

"Fiancée? The elevator doesn't reach the top floor with you, does it?"

116

It's out of my mouth before I can stop it, and I know I made a big mistake.

In two long strides, he makes his way to the side of the bed and lifts me while holding my hair at the nape of my neck, pulling hard.

I tense my muscles, prepared for the incoming punch or slap, but he doesn't hit me like I expect. Nor is there crazed rage in his eyes. He's still perfectly calm.

"They called Jesus crazy too," he comments. "The filthy heretics, those who would see sin control the world, those who would rather rot in Hell in order to revel in their madness and wickedness on Earth. The liars, thieves, whores. There are more of them than ever, and the reason being is those of us who are holy no longer employ the methods of conversion that used to work."

Now his eyes gleam, just a bit, but this is more religious mania than anything I saw before.

"However, here, we believe in a classic approach." He half-drags me by the hair out of the bed and into the bathroom, turning on the water in the tub and letting it fill. He leans me over it, pressing my diaphragm into the hard edge. "Stay still."

There's a noise I can't ever forget: the sound of a belt being undone. I squeeze my eyes shut, just praying it is over soon.

My body still remembers the feeling of a belt hitting my flesh, and I don't even flinch when Thomas strikes straight across my back. And again. Over and over, but not the way Mike used to beat me, uncontrolled and angry, only wanting me to be cowed and under his thumb.

Thomas' whipping feels more like he is trying to maximize my pain: he knows where to hit, how hard, how many times.

My skin is raw and tender, but I won't cry. I stopped crying at this sort of treatment long ago. If he thinks he will break me by beating me, he is sadly mistaken.

He stops when the tub is filled a little over halfway and the belt clatters to the floor.

A strong hand is on the back of my head and before I register what's happening, Thomas plunges my head under the freezing cold water.

I go to gasp air but it's too late, and I wind up with a mouthful of water, choking on it. Drowning.

He lifts me out of the tub and I take in air after spitting out water. When I feel his arm move, I know this time to inhale deeply before my face is plunged back under water.

He holds me longer this time; maybe he knows I grabbed more air before he put me under. I can't hold my breath much longer. I'm going to pass out and drown as my head gets lighter and my chest constricts.

Just as I am ready to give up, he lifts me back out again and I take deep breaths, gripping the edge of the tub to ground me.

Once more, and I am not ready this time, sure I accidentally signed my death warrant. But he doesn't keep me under enough to kill me, once more lifting me as I am sure I will pass out.

My wet hair clings to my face and neck, an added weight; goosebumps pebble my skin from the freezing cold water. My lungs hurt, my chest hurts, and my head spins, even when I close my eyes.

"Let this be a reminder, little sinner, while you're here and breathing, it is because God deems it worthy."

And what if God decides to tell him it's not worth it to keep me breathing?

Thomas lifts me, plopping me still clothed into the frigid water, which comes up to cover just half of me. My bent knees and my chest are exposed to air. And the shock of cold all over my body does nothing for the fact I already couldn't catch my breath.

"However, right now, this is all you are worth."

His zipper rasps and I close my eyes, sure I know what's coming now. Or, rather, I know he's coming now.

But once more his actions shock me, and definitely not in a good way as a warm stream of liquid washes over my exposed chest, breasts clearly visible through the thin white nightgown.

You have got to be fucking with me.

Now I truly want to cry; I don't think I've ever been so demeaned as to be pissed on, but I can't. I have to stay firm. This is day one. What the Hell will day two bring?

When he's done, the zipper rasps again and he says, "Clean yourself up and get to bed. We have a long, long journey to go on, you and I."

CHAPTER TEN

Diana

HELL IS EMPTY, and all the devils are here. Shakespeare said that, and I think he might be right.

When I wake up the morning after being pissed on and nearly drowned, Thomas has a tray of breakfast at my bedside, but his eyes are on me, gaze hard.

"Come here, little sinner," he beckons.

Reluctantly, I stand, seeing something in his hand but I can't really tell what. A small airplane bottle of liquor, maybe?

"Open your mouth and stick out your tongue," he commands.

Before I can stop myself, I comment, "If your plan is to gag me and make me vomit, don't waste your time. You may be delighted to know I have no gag reflex." Turns out I lost it after the gangrape. Funny.

He cocks his head, blond ponytail moving to sit on his shoulder as he does. "Why would I wish to make you sick to your stomach?" He must decide my answer doesn't matter, because he continues, "I have no interest in your lack of gag reflex … yet. Now do as I say and I won't be forced to punish you more than I am about to."

For what? What did I even do while I was asleep?

But I stand and do as he asks. He pinches my tongue between his thumb and forefinger.

"If you attempt to bite me, I guarantee what happened yesterday will feel like a day at the spa. Are we understood?"

I nod as well as I can.

"One of the rules here is extremely basic and simple: you will not curse. None of us do, myself included. Granted, you did not know that, so I will be lenient. Only four drops will be

applied to your tongue."

Four drops…

Fuck my life, that little bottle in

his hand is hot sauce. I don't even know

what kind; there's a burning skull on the

black label. I don't know how I handle

spicy foods. During my time on my

own, I tried a lot of foods I could afford,

but never anything hot.

Thomas' green eyes hold my

gaze as he pours four generous drops on

my tongue, holding it out so the sauce

sinks into the nerve endings.

At first, I feel nothing, and then

the burning begins, activating every

nerve in my mouth and making my eyes

water. The longer it sits on my tongue,

the more intense it gets, until it begins to numb, even as it stings.

Finally, after what feels like ages, he lets my tongue go and I make the mistake of swallowing the remainder of the hot sauce, setting my throat ablaze as I cough. Even my nose is stuffy now, and I wonder how someone managed to bottle lava.

"Be good, Diana, and that never needs to happen again."

Spoiler alert: it happens again.
Not often. I do my best to answer
anything Thomas asks with minimal
words, but once in a while, a curse slips,
and there comes the hot sauce. And
unlike other acquired tastes like coffee
or strong cheese, I don't get any more
used to it than I was the first time.

Thomas keeps me on a rigid
schedule, and I am able to keep track of
days, then weeks, in my mind without
forgetting. I always know when it is
Sunday, because he wakes me up earlier
so he can get to church.

I receive regular meals, can bathe
daily, and receive daily beatings as well.
Twice more Thomas has used me as a
personal urinal. Every time when he has

finished hurting me, there's a disconnect between his body and brain. His eyes look dull and bored, like this is business as usual. But his cock is always at attention, rock hard, as if he gets off on tormenting me.

He hasn't made me bleed yet, and left no scars. Nor has he asked about the few burn marks on my arm. He hasn't seen the hysterectomy scar yet, but an undamaged woman would have a period by now. If he doesn't ask about it now, he will soon. I have a feeling he's an intelligent, well-read man, albeit a nutty one. He isn't going to forget about that.

I hope he will accept the base truth of, "I can't have periods." If he makes me speak of my past, that is what will break me. That will be my undoing.

I built these walls inside my mind, and the voice of my conscience protects them. If they were to fall, if I had to face my past, I would collapse along with said walls. He has asked me a few times about my years on the street, and I give basic answers for that as well. No hints I was anywhere else before. Nothing about my life.

If he knows my name, he likely knows I am an orphan, which could be another reason he took me. No one would come looking. Mike isn't on any official paperwork, just what he forged to be my "guardian" to pull me out of school and ensure CPFS didn't come after him.

For all intents and purposes, let Thomas believe I was on my own since my mom died.

But he doesn't. He asks me too often; he knows I'm lying. And that's when the beatings get worse. Last night, his silence was more frightening than him threatening me. I had been equally silent when he asked me about the last few years, and when he stopped trying, there was this calculating look in his eyes that freaked me out. Like he was planning something.

Now, today, I haven't seen him. A young guy not much older than me has brought my meals, never once looking at or speaking to me.

Funny, I'm eating more. Thomas informed me he added some sort of protein powder to my breakfast every day. I don't know why my weight was such a concern for him, though. And no way in Hell am I going to ask.

I'm just biding my time until I can get out of here.

He seems to want to let me out. He calls me his fiancée and says God sent me to him to "save". So if I play along and let him save me, I can go back to my life, right?

What life? my conscience whispers. *You'll have lost your apartment and ruined the meager credit you built*

*because of unpaid bills by the time you're
out of this basement. You'll be beyond
square one.*

I squeeze my eyes shut. I can
make it. I made it before with less than
nothing, I can do it again.

Even if the thought of really
giving in and succumbing to this life
with Thomas sometimes sounds
tempting.

In the darkness of night, after he
has shut the lights and all that filters in
is weak moonlight from the sealed
window near the ceiling, my mind
wanders. To how it would feel to give
in, to let him save me. To have a home,
food, not be forced to fuck anyone.

Would he stop hurting me if I agreed to his terms?

Would he be a good person?

Am I fucking nuts for thinking any of this?

That last question at least I can answer with a resounding "YES".

As I think, the door opens and Thomas walks in, carrying a metal rod of some sort and a set of cuffs that match the one on my ankle.

My eyes widen, but I do my best to remain still. My whole body wants to run, to cower away, because there's only one place I can imagine him putting that thing.

Stay firm, my mind whispers. *Don't give him your sadness, your fear, your pain. He doesn't deserve it.*

"Diana, lean forward and place your hands on top of the foot of the bed," Thomas commands.

I nod and move, but apparently too slowly for him, because he grabs my wrists in one large hand and holds them to the metal bar atop the footboard, quickly securing the cuffs as if he's had practice.

He positions me as if I am a doll, and my body reacts by allowing my mind to retreat within itself. I wondered many times when he'd rape me, shocked every day that went by when he didn't.

I knew he wasn't any different, I knew this was just a matter of when, not if.

Yet, a small part of my heart that wanted to believe he wouldn't do this breaks, and I curse it. How fucking stupid and childish to have thought a man, or anyone, would be decent to me?

The front of my nightgown tears between his hands, rending it in two. It falls down my shoulders and he pushes it away, letting the torn pieces sit around my waist. It looks like I'm planking with my bare tits swaying in the breeze.

He walks over to me, still stone-faced, and rubs my dangling breasts.

First he sort of massages them, then he begins to pull on my nipples.

For a moment, I feel desire stir deep inside and tamp it down before it can grow into a wildfire. Am I insane? I haven't felt actual desire … ever? Maybe before Mike started molesting me, I felt some adolescent version of it, but since then? Nothing.

Now I get off, apparently, on being abused. Fucking aces.

He begins to pull too hard, and I whimper as pain shoots through me, right to my betraying cunt. I am so stupid. So damaged. So broken. This nutcase thinks he can save me? I'm so beyond God's grace.

"Men were always drawn to your oversized breasts, were they not?" he asks me.

"Yes, sir," I say, voice dull.

"And they're real?"

I nod. "Yes, sir."

"Are you proud of them, little sinner?"

"No," I reply. "I just used them to make money."

He releases one nipple and holds the other out, stretching my breast and holding it aloft. "These are meant for your loyal husband, to nurse his children and for him to touch and abuse as he pleases. No one else. These have caused you to corrupt innocent men, and in turn corrupt yourself. *Apologize!*"

As he shouts the last word, his free hand forms into a fist and punches my taut breast hard. It smacks out of his hand and slaps against me as I bite my lip to keep from shouting in pain.

I refuse to apologize. I never did a damn thing wrong. It was the world that did me wrong.

"You need this. Your tits deserve this. A reminder of how vile you've behaved." He hits them a few more times with his bare fists, the force making my chest and diaphragm ache.

What if he breaks my ribs?

But he stops and picks up the metal rod … or is that a cane?

He looks at it for a moment and my whole body tenses up. I'm not ready for this. If he rapes me with it, that will be what breaks me irreparably. He taps it against his open palm and says, "I should penetrate you with this. Feel the cold, unyielding steel as it rearranges your insides. That's what you *deserve*, however I feel as if that would just excite you more, heathen."

So … he's not?

"You should begin to pray. For forgiveness, for salvation, and in gratitude." That is all the warning he gives me before the metal cane whacks against the soft skin of my breasts. On top, across my nipples, underneath as he holds each one up in turn by the nipples.

The pain is so bad you could set me on fire and I'd feel it less. Beads of blood pool below the surface of my skin, and the sensitive area is already beginning to bruise. I can't look away, despite the repulsion roiling through me.

Eventually I fade back into my own subconscious, tuning out the pain and his deep grunts as much as I can. Strands of hair come loose from his ponytail, dangling in his face. His cheeks are flushed as well, but his eyes are as dead as ever.

Eventually, he stops, and the cane clatters to the floor.

He unhooks the cuffs and my body flops down on the mattress, and I immediately regret doing that, as it aggravates my brand new wounds.

Thomas roughly turns me over so I am on my back, bare tits bouncing. As soon as I see his hand on his belt, I look away, but I can see him from the periphery of my vision.

I learned the hard way men want to be seen, to not close my eyes when they use me, so I don't.

He takes his rock hard cock out, stroking it. It's thick and long, precum at the tip. I wonder where he's going to put it first, how bad he'll hurt me like everyone else.

But he doesn't move closer.

He keeps stroking, staring at my wounded breasts, until he starts speaking. I can't understand it, and search my brain for what language it could be before I realize it's not a language. He's praying, speaking in tongues.

Oh, he really is so psychotic.

His voice gets deeper, melodic, faster. Even as he gasps and covers my breasts in warm semen, he doesn't stop until he is completely spent. Breathing hard, his eyes look more human now. Pupils wide, sparkles in them. When he meets my eyes, I look away.

Thomas says nothing, merely tucks himself back into his jeans, zips, buckles his belt, and leaves.

Leaving me bruised, wounded, covered in sticky come.

When the door shuts behind him

with a soft snick of the lock, I finally let

myself cry.

CHAPTER ELEVEN

Thomas

I LEAVE DIANA after relieving my aching balls all over those beautiful, bruised breasts. Just thinking how the colors will deepen to a kaleidoscope of red, purple, and green by tomorrow could make me hard again.

This was my biggest challenge yet since joining the community. Could I do what I needed to do, despite knowing it would arouse me, without taking her? Without making her mine, without forcing her to worship me as she should? Could I prove I changed from the man I used to be before I joined?

And I passed the test. I proved myself. I proved that my transformation was nearly complete, that God worked within me since arriving here. Despite temptation, I did not succumb.

Diana is so beautiful. So strong yet fragile. I see the sweetness below the hardened exterior her life on the streets caused her to build around her heart. I just need to figure out how else to reach her. I need a bridge of sorts.

I have applied the physical aspects, but she seems to reject anything emotional. Something has to bridge it, to make her more comfortable with me.

As usual when I have issues to work out, I go to one of two people in whom I find it easy to confide: my older sister, Lisa.

Typically, I would have used her to let out my frustration and arousal, as unmarried people within the compound serve this purpose. But now that I have found Diana, the thought of touching anyone — even someone as beautiful as my sister — makes me feel sick to my stomach.

I find her at the church, practicing with the choir. Mother Catherine, Father Oliver's wife, directs them, while he plays the piano.

Normally I would speak to Father

Oliver about any issues I have, but I

need a woman's touch.

When they finish their song,

Mother Catherine calls for a break and

my sister spots me immediately, coming

to sit in the pew next to me as she

downs her water.

"What brings you by? Ready to

sing with us?" She nudges me playfully.

"I'll leave the hymns to the choir

and focus on my sermons," I reply.

"Actually, I wanted your advice, as my

sister, not as a church member."

Nodding, she leans back in the

pew. "Of course. I assume it's about

your little plaything in the basement?"

"Diana is my *fiancée*, not a toy," I scold her.

"Right, right. Sorry. Anyway, what's up?"

I sigh, toying with my ponytail. This is out of my depth entirely. "I need something to balance out the punishment and training. Diana has stopped talking back, mostly stopped cursing, and is generally responding well. She is even eating better. She deserves something but the reward part of 'punish and reward' … eludes me."

Lisa chuckles. "You know, women really aren't that mysterious." She holds out her hand, showing her manicure. "We like cosmetics, soft things, nice smells…"

"Are you saying my house stinks?" I arch an eyebrow at her.

"No! I'm saying that basement is bare and uncomfortable and sterile. Give her something cute, something soft, something that isn't monochrome," Lisa explains. "Home comforts while she is in your home. At least for now, until her training is over and she can come upstairs."

I smile at my sister. "Thank you. I should have thought of that myself."

She rolls her eyes. "I was always the socially smart sibling. You had your books to tend to." She stands and pats my shoulder. "Good luck with her. If you ask me, God gave you quite the challenge, Pastor-in-Training."

He has. But I trust God sent me Diana for a reason, to help me grow and to help save the woman my soul was made for.

I head back home and double check Diana's ID for her address in the city before I drive over in a bit. It's about an hour away and in a neighborhood that must once have been nice, but the pandemic, inflation, and the wicked ways of our politicians have caused it to fall into disrepair, according to a quick Google search.

A shame.

Sister Lisa said home comforts; I must agree the basement is bare. And Diana has behaved the past three weeks. She is owed something.

Also, she has bills that will accumulate. I should go settle things with her landlord, electric company, things like that. After I ensure Diana has been brought lunch, I head to the address on her ID, wrinkling my nose at the location once I arrive. I feel as if I may get stabbed just getting out of my car.

The six-flat is derelict, and that's being polite. Once Diana has earned it and I can take her out of the basement, I'm sure she will love my little lakeside home much better than this Hellhole.

The front door isn't even locked; I enter it easily. Her apartment is on the top floor, to the left. The little pink rabbit keychain reminds me I made the

right choice with her. This bit of whimsy
and childlike wonder means she can still
be saved.

Unlocking her door, the
apartment looks barely lived in at all.
Threadbare carpet, walls once white,
now gray, a window facing the
gangway, and worn, old furniture. Not
even a TV. Nothing to suggest comfort
whatsoever. Except the pile of ratty,
secondhand books against one wall.
Peering closer, they are all Young Adult
fantasy and paranormal; some classics.
My girl apparently likes to read.

In the bathroom, the nicest thing
in there appears to be cosmetics. I take
the facial cleansers and body wash,
putting them into a bag I brought with

me. They could be used to bargain with her as well.

The kitchen is more well-used, but the food in there is scant, cheap, and generic. My nose involuntarily wrinkles.

Finally, her bedroom. This looks like a room she took care of. The bed doesn't look new, but the mattress is high, and the worn sheets look comfortable. So does the pile of pillows and 2 plush toys. There are posters of some pop star on the walls.

The TV is in here, facing the bed. It's small, looks more like a desktop monitor than a TV.

Inside the closet, none of these clothes can be salvaged. My future wife can't be seen in ratty, cut-up t-shirts and

certainly not in the clothes she wore
while streetwalking. Those can be burnt.
The others can be donated, whatever
isn't cut up or full of holes. I make notes
in my phone; I will send some of the
church ladies over. I'm sure Sister Lisa
can spare some of them for a day to help
pack up and donate things.

Home comforts.

I'm a man who needs little,
always have been. But I know many
who need collectibles and things like
that to feel comfortable. Diana has
earned something.

Leaning across her bed, I grab
one of the two stuffed toys: a ratty, old
red and black gingham bear with
mismatched white button eyes and a

badly sewn-on nose. Its mouth gives a friendly, lopsided smile. The rabbit that matches the keychain can stay. This thing looks much more … loved.

"Diana?" a woman's trembling voice calls. "Diana, thank God! It's been three weeks, I was worried something happened to you—" The woman cuts off as I enter the living room, her face turning ghost white.

Diana was angry with me; never once these past three weeks have I seen fear on her face. I don't want her to fear me; no one should be in fear of another human.

This woman? The word petrified would not be enough to describe what I see in her eyes. And there is a green

bruise on her face that makeup can't
hide.

"I'm sorry, I—"

"Wait," I call, wishing my voice
wasn't naturally deep and commanding.
I don't want to scare this woman
further.

She turns to me, visibly
trembling.

"Diana is my fiancée," I tell her.
"I was just getting a few things for her."
I hold up the bag and doll.

She looks less scared now; more
sad and despondent as tears come to her
eyes. Looking away from me, she nods.
"I'm glad she's getting out of this
Hellhole. I hope she never sets foot here
again. Can you … can you tell her I said

thank you for protecting Whitney and helping me out when she could?"

"Protecting?" I ask. Shaking my head, I decide I will ask Diana. "Of course I'll tell her, Miss?" I pause, waiting for her to give her name.

"Thompson. Mrs. Thompson. My husband passed but I still prefer missus," she explains, raising her eyes to meet mine. "Congratulations to you both. But if I may, ensure you cancel her lease if you haven't already. Rick will come after her for lost money."

"Rick is the landlord?"

She shivers. "Not surprised Diana never mentioned him. Anyway, I need to figure some things out, I'm sorry. Congratulations again!" She scurries away, hunched over as if preparing for an attack.

Something doesn't sit right with me, and I need to have a talk with my fiancée.

Back at home, I go right down to the basement and knock on the door before I open it, finding Diana sitting on the edge of the bed, looking off into the distance. Sometimes when she does this, she looks pained. Today, however, she looks happy. I almost wish I didn't have to disturb her.

"Diana."

At her name, she jumps and turns towards me, watching me with wary eyes.

"I have questions for you." I shut the door and walk towards her, shocked when she doesn't flinch, just moves over to let me sit. Good. I don't want her scared of me. What I do is for her own good. I think, deep down, she knows that.

"First … I brought you something," I admit, reaching into the bag to pull out the teddy bear.

Her hard, wary eyes fill with tears, and I see the girl she once was, the woman she could be. Whatever happened in between those two periods to bring her to the life I saved her from, I hope to erase it completely.

She nearly snatches the bear from me, clutching it to her chest, as tears fall down her sweet face.

"I went to your old apartment," I admit.

For the first time, I see terror in her eyes. "Why would you— Wait. You mean where I live now?"

"Lived," I correct, mentally tabling another discussion I will need to have with her. Where on Earth did she live before? Was she not with family? "You live here now."

She clutches the bear tighter to her chest, no longer looking at me. Ah well. In time she will come to think of my home as her home. As soon as I finish my work with her.

"I ran into someone there, a Mrs. Thompson."

Her eyes widen, but still she doesn't look at me. "Is she okay? What about Whitney, her daughter?"

"She didn't look well, and appeared to panic when I said you wouldn't be returning," I say. "She told me to thank you for protecting her daughter, and she was glad you got out of that building."

Diana is silent.

"What goes on there that you needed to protect her child?" I press.

She shakes her head so hard her hair flies.

I nudge the bag with the cosmetics closer. "Let's cooperate here. It's not anything you did wrong, is it?"

She shakes her head again.

I push the bag even closer to her. "I brought you something else from home."

With a side-eyed glance, as if I'll bite, she peers inside, her pretty mouth forming a little O shape.

"Tell me exactly what went on in your apartment, and you can have these, too."

"You need to believe me…" She trails off for a second. "There's nothing you can do."

"Let me be the judge of that."

"You don't get it." Her voice is hard, angry, hurt. "I tell you, you will go to the police. And they'll pretend to investigate, and Rick will … no. *No.* I won't make things any worse for them!"

"Diana. Look at me."

She does, determination aflame in her eyes. I would never tell her, but I love that look. As much as I want to break her, I must do so carefully. This spark is one I will love in my wife. I do not wish for meek and submissive always. Submissive to me in many ways, yes, but never meek in such a way as she has no personality.

Sometimes even *I* like to play with fire.

"Do you believe I would go to the police when they may come here to question me? I do not know this Rick person, but I am sure he would, as most other heathens, happily throw me to the wolves to save his own skin." I gesture to her. "I know what I have done is not wrong. The law sees things in black and white, not shades of gray."

She is silent, so I continue.

"It seems he has done horrible things; he should be punished. But only you can help me do that. Consider this part of your training. To trust in me, and to condemn those within your past."

"I need you to make me a promise. You won't let Whitney or her mom be hurt." Her eyes soften.

"Please."

That word shocks me to my core.
I have put her through three weeks of
my restructural training for her body
and soul, and never once has she
begged for anything. Yet, on someone
else's behalf, she lowers herself to
pleading.

"I promise."

She sighs and sits back, so her
back is against the bare stone wall, still
clutching the bear for dear life.

"He is assigned to the public aid
office and Section 8. For poor people,"
she adds, as if I don't know what that is.
"He is marked as a safe space for young
women and mothers. He's not."

Her eyes turn dull; so sudden, it startles me.

"When I moved in, it was about ten months ago now, I didn't have much. And the lease *said* we got three days leeway for late rent. Well … he wanted it that night, when he showed up at my apartment, letting himself in with his keys." She glances at me and then away. "I'm sure you can guess what happened next."

My stomach churns. There is a reason aside from wanting her body and soul equally cleansed that I have not properly had sex with her. When I'm inside her, I need her to beg me for it first. I need her to want me as much as I want her, if not more. I have absolutely no interest in laying with a woman whose heart doesn't feel the same, nor her body. Not anymore, anyway.

She will desire me first.

I nod at her words. "And the neighbors?"

"He beat Mrs. Thompson while Whitney was in school. He said next time, he'd … he'd rape Whitney. She's twelve, for fuck's sake!"

I ignore her curse for the moment over my own disgust. The Bible is very clear on one thing: harming a child is a direct insult to God.

"I took her to my apartment the next afternoon after Mrs. Thompson said she was short two hundred dollars so she would be safe. Lied that Whitney wasn't going to be home until the next day. He said if she didn't have the money within a day, there would be nowhere the kid could hide."

She bends her knees and tucks her head, and the bear, into them. "That was the night you picked me up."

"You were working to earn the two hundred dollars?" I ask.

She nods, a tear slipping down her cheek.

I catch it with my hand and she flinches, but I press my palm to her face. My soft touches make her flinch, yet she doesn't bend or break when I inflict pain. Interesting.

I wonder about what she just said to me. Did I inadvertently cause a child to come to harm?

"You are a good person, Diana," I assure her. "That is why I am keeping you here, washing away the stain of all the sin so that goodness can shine."

I stand up, placing the bag of cosmetics on the bed next to her. "Thank you for trusting me with this information."

"What will you do?" she asks me.

"Make it right." I cannot undo what has already been done, but I can change the course of the future.

But first, I have to get the hot sauce from the cupboard. After all, my

dove did curse, and I cannot be lenient
on her.

CHAPTER TWELVE

Thomas

I LEAVE DIANA some water — I do not
need her throat damaged because she
accidentally inhaled the hot sauce when
I only meant to drizzle it on her tongue
— and ensure she is locked in before I
go to the rectory attached to our church,
where Father Oliver and his wife spend
most of their days.

Mother Catherine lets me in, her
reddish curls bouncing as always. She is

our success story for rescuing spouses; so different from the junkie Oliver told us about.

Oliver, an albino man with dignified white hair in a ponytail, is about ten years older than I, but he seems much more worldly than I could ever dream of being. He sits at a chair in his office, writing. No doubt for his sermon or the church's blog.

"Brother Thomas, what brings you here this evening?" he asks me in his pleasant, lilting Irish accent. "Did everything go smoothly at Diana's apartment?"

I shake my head. "Not … exactly. Do you have time to converse, Father?"

He nods. "Of course, I always have time for my fellows within the church. We are here as a family, after all."

Catherine asks, "Can I bring you anything?"

"No, dear. If we need something, we will tell you," Oliver says.

"Mother," I interject, "I was wondering if you and Sister Lisa could organize some ladies to go and get Diana's things packed within the next week? Anything suitable, we can donate to the women's shelter."

She nods, eyes alight. "What a lovely idea."

"Also … she has a pile of ratty books. Can someone take down the authors and titles for me?"

Once more, her curls bounce as she nods. "Of course, Brother Thomas. She is quite lucky to have you, isn't she?"

I smile. "And once I am done working with her soul, we will be lucky to have her, too." I wait for Catherine to leave before I speak. I am sure what she did as an addict, nothing would shock her, but I wish to spare her the details of what Diana told me.

"So, Brother, what is it you need? You look troubled," Oliver says.

"Diana's landlord may have harmed a child the night after I brought

Diana here," I admit. "Because I took her, that may be partially my fault."

Oliver regards me carefully. "We cannot stop things set in motion, you know this. I wouldn't be so hasty as to blame yourself."

I nod. "I realize that, but I am but human, Father. I wish to assuage my guilt."

"We will help you as we can. What did you require?"

"Brother Joseph, whom you said helped change Catherine's information to keep her safe, I'd like him to assign that building to me. I will own it from now on."

Oliver nods. "I trust you will ensure the current landowner will not put up a struggle?"

I smile. "Oh, I hope he struggles at least a little."

The popular idiom is, if one kills a killer, the amount of killers in the world remains the same. Not so.

If one kills many killers, the amount of killers in the world diminishes. Some philosophers should

178

at least attend math class a few times. And if one kills those who would harm innocent women and children … I consider that pest extermination.

"Well, well, look what the cat dragged in."

Hank sits behind a battered desk, his dirt-crusted boots on top of probably important paperwork, hands behind his head. His lank, greasy hair hangs loose in his face. He added a neck tattoo since I last saw him. No one would guess this man is a multi-millionaire.

Nor would they guess that about me, I suppose.

"How's the funny farm treating you and Lisa?"

I grin at him, tossing hair from my face. "Lisa settled in faster than I did, but I admit it's a nice life. Better than this one."

"And yet you still darkened my doorstep. What the fuck do you want?" Despite his coarse words, his tone is friendly. Lisa and I are the only people to leave Hank's organization and live. He can use some good, upstanding church members to back him up if the cops ever come calling. And they will, eventually. He gave us a pretty good living, so we won't hesitate to help him.

"How much to have you clean up after me tonight?"

"You taking contracts again? The church allows that?"

I shake my head. "There's a man taking advantage of vulnerable women and children. I need him gone. As part of my penance, to ensure I am worthy of my fiancée."

Hank's eyes flare. "Free. Just call me as usual when you're done. Fucker hurting kids, I hope you make it last long, Tommy."

I grin, going to the hidden cupboard in the far left wall for my weapon. "Oh, trust me, I plan on it."

It's been five days since I got Oliver's permission to take care of Rick. I had to wait until Joe hacked into the city's files and created a sale transfer of the building deed into my name.

I didn't cancel Diana's lease. I want him angry, and there at midnight, just like what he did to her before. I need to look him in the eyes as he sees the Earthly punishment God has sent upon him.

Inside the apartment, I sit on the edge of her still unmade bed, calm. My heart rate is normal, my breathing even. Even my nerves do not thrum. The adrenaline will hit soon enough, but for now I am at peace with what I am doing; I am in the right.

I check the time on my phone and quickly shut the screen so no light emerges from under the closed bedroom door.

Twelve-oh-one.

Right on time, the front door of the apartment rattles, and locks turn. The sound is as loud as a gunshot in the silence.

"Diana!" Rick's abrasive voice cuts through the still. I nearly flinch at the sound; not something I would typically admit to. It appears I'm a bit rusty. "Who the fuck do you think you are trying to skip out on rent, you little whore? The fuckin' bums you suck off for two dollars didn't pay you enough?"

There it is. My rage. Like an old friend, my rage and I have a long history, and it reminds me it exists every so often. Like when I am forced to beat Diana. It takes the edge off.

But it has been some time since I truly let the blackness out to play. Two years since there last was blood on my hands and peace in my soul.

I will remedy that tonight, and allow my rage to go back into its uneasy slumber.

The bedroom door opens, and the light flicks on.

Rick — a tall, nearly emaciated man with wisps of hair and an ill-fitting suit — stands in the threshold, staring at me in disbelief.

"You're not — where is Diana Hill?" he barks, trying to cover up his discomfort. "If you're her fuckin' John, I told her not to bring it here to this damn building, so get the Hell out before I—"

"Oh, will you *shut up*?" I ask, standing to my full height. He's taller, but I am fitter, and if I may say so, more imposing. "You're the landlord?" I need to be sure before I go further.

"Yeah, and your whore is late on her rent!"

I nod, running a hand through my hair. "First of all, Diana is not my whore, she is my fiancée. Second, she owes you nothing on account of the fact she doesn't live here, and you no longer own this building."

"What nonsense are you talking about?" he asks.

"I own it now. And I dispersed the rest of your assets to other reputable landowners or sold them off; the profits will go into local women's shelters to protect them from predators like you. Now, one more question."

Rick stammers as I speak, clearly in shock, and likely he is unsure if he should believe me.

"Did you touch the child?"

"What?"

"Did. You. Touch. Whitney. Thompson?" I grind every word out, my patience dancing on a razor's edge. It will be cut at any moment, and I need his answer before that happens.

"What's it to you?"

"It means nothing to me," I lie. "But your answer is the catalyst between two things: fast or slow."

Another lie. I will need to sit down with Father Oliver after this to cleanse my soul. I have already decided it will be slow, unless he makes too much noise.

"Fast or…"

"My patience will snap at any given moment. I suggest you answer the question."

"No. The bitch mother said she's on vacation with her father's family. But she can't stay away forever. Why? Did you want a go too?"

Darkness descends upon my vision, sight narrowing down on the evil, disgusting creature before me.

Swiftly, I bend to the knife holster on my boot and produce a decent-sized dagger, my preferred weapon of choice. I have used various guns, poison, my bare hands, kitchen knives, and one memorable time, a baseball bat with a screwdriver head attached. But this specific dagger feels right in my hands as I mete out justice on God's behalf.

"I would say I'll see you in Hell, but I am honestly unsure if Satan will take you."

Rick looks at the dagger and turns to run, but my rage has snapped, making my every movement precise and fluid. Unlike others when they give in to their instinct, I do not become unraveled and uncontrolled. Rather, it is the opposite. Every sense is sharpened like an animal, and like one, I take my prey with deliberate, quick movements, ensuring I have time to play with it.

Yanking him back by his collar, I relish the fear in his beady eyes and smile. Everything moves in perfect slow motion, allowing me to handle my first thrust effortlessly, into his nonexistent stomach.

He gasps and doubles over, legs unsteady as he tries to cover the wound, but my blade is too wide for his hands to properly cover it all, not with the way I cut. Blood seeps between his fingers, staining his already rumpled and dirty shirt. He looks at me in disbelief, and I smile and shrug before I grab his jacket in one hand and continue to stab him.

Over and over and over again.

The blade cleanly renders flesh, sliding into his body as if I were cutting through cotton candy, if the confectionery could bleed, that is.

My rage controls the thrusts, never going too far so as to harm me or make me lose my grip on the cretin. I am unsure if I have blinked lately. It doesn't feel like it, but that doesn't matter.

Rick gurgles as he tries to scream, to give voice to the intense agony I am sure he must feel at the moment, as his insides have been shredded to ribbons, intestines trailing along his thighs, hitting his knees like cut rope. The smell of copper fills the room, a perfume to my senses.

Blood pours from his mouth, and he meets my eyes.

"Why?"

The word is barely intelligible, but I have heard it enough from my victims to know what he said. It amuses me to no end that those who commit the worst atrocities see themselves as some sort of heroes and cannot fathom why anyone would want to slowly slice them up as if they were a Sunday roast.

The evil always believe they are doing the work of God.

"Because I cannot suffer your sort of sin to live." I let go, slightly shoving him back so he lays prostrate on Diana's old bed. "While I am sure God has turned His ears from your pleas, if you wish to pray, you had best begin now."

His eyes are glassy; he will die soon.

I won't allow him to pass peacefully. No, he will look into the eyes of his redeemer.

Leaning over him, I ensure he can see me before I grin, waving the dagger before his gaze.

And then I plunge it into his blood-clogged throat, slicing quickly, barely avoiding the spray of blood from his carotid. I think some may have gotten in my hair.

I stand before the corpse, breathing hard, noting a wet patch in the front of his pants. I will never cease to find the way the dead cannot hold their bowels or bladder disgusting.

Undignified.

I use Diana's duvet to wipe the majority of the blood from the blade before I re-sheath it. Mother Catherine will clean it completely for me before I return it to Hank's office. Discarding one of the black gloves I wore, I text Hank the address and a bomb emoji. It's our code to "explode" the evidence.

With my still-gloved hand, I go into Rick's pants pocket and find his wallet soaked in blood. His ID is stained around the edges. I take it with me as I head home.

As always, adrenaline surges through me after a kill, tightening my pants and making my heart beat stronger. It is a gamble going to see Diana now. I may not be able to control myself in front of her, and it is not yet time for me to claim her as mine in the flesh.

I check to make sure my boots have no blood on them — they don't — before I enter my home and head down to the basement. It is past one in the morning, but Diana is awake, humming, holding the bear in one arm against her chest.

How beautiful she looks, more innocent than she is. My cock insists I take her now, but I must restrain myself, or I will undo all the work I began within her. I am no longer the man I once was, and I need to remember that. As alluring as she is, as much as my darkness demands the feel of her soft flesh beneath me, I must resist.

Being the junior pastor has its perks in that I have my pick of single women within the community to take my passions out on should I require it, though I typically choose Lisa. I'm most comfortable with her, seeing as I've known her my entire life. However, I don't *want* her.

I want the sweet, strong, beautiful creature in the bed before me.

Diana looks at me and her eyes widen. Does she see blood? The bulge my black jeans will not hide?

I wait as I stand at the side of her bed, wondering what she will say.

"You're wearing all black."

Huh. That was not what I expected. "Yes, I am."

"Is ... there a reason?"

I nod, handing her the blood-speckled driver's license. "Yes. I only wear black when I need to hide the bloodstains."

CHAPTER THIRTEEN

Diana

I BARELY HEAR Thomas' knock; I'm too busy singing inside my mind, trying to calm myself as cabin fever still itches at the edge of my sanity.

I hate this. And yet … despite what he's done to me, this is the safest I have ever been since Dad died.

The irony.

When I hear Thomas' boots stop at my bedside, I look up at him and do a double take. If this was one of my beloved books, I'd say he had an evil twin.

I've never seen him in anything less formal than black trousers and a lightweight, usually white, button-down shirt, with his hair tied back, away from his face.

This man, with beautiful, wild blond curls let loose, in black jeans, motorcycle boots, shirt, and leather jacket, is a stranger. There is blood in his hair and a tent in his pants.

Blood.

I should be terrified.

All I am is curious. Especially since he just stares at me, not speaking.

"You're wearing all black."

He blinks, as if surprised at my words. "Yes, I am."

"Is ... there a reason?" That's only part of my question. I want to know why he's in black, why his whole demeanor has changed, and especially why there is blood in his curls.

He nods and pulls something from his pocket, holding it out to me.

I take it, eyes widening. It's Rick's driver's license, and it is covered in barely dried blood.

"Yes," Thomas answers, his voice a deep rasp. "I only wear black when I need to hide the bloodstains." His intense green eyes stare down at me and it's like I can read his mind.

He hasn't looked at me sexually at all since he brought me down here, even when he got hard after tormenting me. Not even when he came on me. Now, it's different. A part of me wants to cry, knowing the one thing that set him apart from everyone else I ever had to deal with, is now gone.

But he surprises me again as he turns away, walking to the door. As he opens it, he says, "Get some sleep. Sister Lisa will be in tomorrow to see you."

I can barely sleep. My mind keeps whirling, wondering what the fuck happened. Does this ID mean he killed my bastard landlord? What will happen to the building now? The Thompsons can't afford to move.

Eventually I drift off, only to be woken when my door opens.

The beautiful woman I used to see walking with Thomas when I was on the streets enters, followed by another woman, a bit older, with red hair. The woman I recall seeing has a brown paper shopping bag, while the other has a recyclable takeout tray that smells good.

"Good morning, did we wake you?" the pretty woman chirps. Her smile gives me the creeps. It's plastic, as if her real expression would show not happiness, but some sort of malice.

"I, um, yes it's okay," I mumble, rubbing sleep from my eyes. "Can … may I use the bathroom?"

"Of course." The woman with the red hair gestures to the bathroom and I rush in there.

No one has been to see me since Thomas brought me here. I know these two must be with this fucked up church too, but why are they here? I pee and brush my hair, wondering why I feel nothing except mild curiosity.

Maybe because it's unlikely you're going to be raped?

I sigh at my subconscious, but she's right.

Exiting back into the main room of the basement, I see another man walk down the stairs, this one with a thick, dark beard, also wearing mostly white. In fact, only Thomas usually wears dark trousers it seems. Every time I saw any of them in public, the darkest color they wore was beige. Is there a reason, or is he a rebel?

The new man places a small end table with an empty cabinet beneath it next to my bed. He nods to the two women, calling the redhead, "Mother." He doesn't look at me. Is he not supposed to? Because I belong to Thomas? Or because I'm some Godforsaken heathen?

"I don't believe we have formally met," the one called "Mother" says, holding a hand out to me. "My name is Catherine, I am Father Oliver's wife. Once you're indoctrinated into the church completely, you may call me Mother. For now, Catherine will do." She looks me up and down with an approving smile. "You're beautiful; God and Thomas made an excellent choice."

"It would've been nice if I got a choice," I say before I can stop myself.

The pretty woman with the long brown hair and blue eyes glares at me. "The Divine Plan is beyond our wants and needs. I see Thomas still needs to work hard on you. You don't even deserve any of this."

"Sister Lisa," Catherine scolds quietly. She continues to me, "Brother Thomas asked Lisa and I to bring you something to eat from outside, as a celebration of sorts, that one of the men forcing you to sin is out of the picture."

She hands me the takeout tray; it's from a local café I always wanted to try but could never afford.

"And these." Lisa places the bag on the floor at my feet, as if I am not worthy of handing it to directly.

"May I look inside?" I ask, more interested in the bag than the food.

"Yes, but if what Lisa and I saw in your apartment is anything to go by, please ensure your food doesn't go cold as you sort through these." Catherine's smile is sweet.

I peek in the bag and want to sob.

Books. Brand new books!

Some of them I had in my apartment, some I never read before.

Books!

Thomas told them to bring me books?

"You're gonna have to forgive me but … I thought places like this didn't like women to be well-read," I say.

Lisa rolls her eyes. "What good are we to God if only half of us have any knowledge of His world? Besides, I don't think Narnia books are going to radicalize you."

"Tell him thank you for me, please." Whatever brought on the show of kindness, I am smart enough to know I need to be as grateful as I'd be were he to release me.

"You can tell him yourself, later," Catherine says. "Now, please eat. Sort your books in the cabinet as you'd like. It's solid, I doubt you can lift it, but note that if you try to use anything as a weapon, it will be taken away."

My eyes widen. "I'd never use a book as a weapon. I don't want to damage one."

Lisa laughs at that. "Yeah, lob one at Thomas' hard head, it will definitely get damaged."

They leave me, and I want to immediately start organizing my books, but if they return, or if my jailer does, and sees I haven't eaten, I don't want to deal with any sort of punishment.

I open the container and poke at the food, things I read about in books but never had the chance to try my whole life. A celebration that someone who made me sin is gone.

So Thomas killed my evil landlord. I should be terrified of that, of him. All I feel is gratitude. But now I worry about the building, everyone

living there. What will happen to them?
What if the next owner is worse?

There is nothing I can do about it
now. So I do the one thing I can, the one
thing that I loved to do since I was a
child: I read.

But first I organize the ten books I
was given by author name in the small
cabinet, and then sit down on the floor,
back against the bed, and open up *The
Hobbit*.

I don't know how long I read for.
The passage of time is meaningless in
reality, while my mind is elsewhere,
living a whole other life through these
characters. I am not trapped, stuck,
chained in a basement with a religious
cultist who beats me to "save" me. I am

an adventurer, a burglar, fighting a fire-
breathing dragon protecting its stolen
hoard. I am a gentle friend, a brave soul
who ventured far from home to help
someone else retrieve what they lost.

When I read, I am home.

When the door to my dungeon
opens, I jump and realize my ass hurts.

It has to have been hours.

Thomas looks over at me from
the doorway, looking more like his
normal self in a white shirt and jeans —
not black this time — with his hair tied
back. But there is something with his
expression…

He's smiling. And not the polite
smile he gave when I met him on the
street, or the cunning one I often see.

This is a sweet smile you'd give a friend … or a girlfriend.

How could someone who kidnaps, tortures, degrades, and murders look so … cute?

"I see you are enjoying your reward," he says.

"Thank you, I am," I reply.

"Mother Catherine said you have some questions about last night," he continues, sitting on the edge of the bed. "Sit by me, put the book down."

I do as he asks, placing the book on the metal tray where the takeout container, now empty, sits.

"I was wondering … what happens to the building my landlord owns now?"

Thomas cocks his head, as if pondering my question. He does that a lot, as if the things I say or ask don't align with what he expects of me, and yet for these things I am never punished.

"I own that building. And all his other assets were sold to good owners and the money donated to charitable causes," he replies.

"Will you … will you take others like you took me?" The thought of Mrs. Thompson or little Whitney being held here makes me want to vomit.

"You are the only one I want, my little dove." His eyes are hard at the suggestion he'd take anyone else. Obsession shines in them. "I will never replace the gift God sent to me." He places his hand in my hair, gently tugging, as if showing possession.

I wasn't sent to you, I think. *You took me!*

I nod. "Um … thank you. You made sure a lot of people were safe."

He nods, removing his hand from my hair.

"Have you … ever worried about yourself? Since you arrived here, while you asked me what I was going to do with you, all you have spoken of are others," Thomas says.

I turn away. "I did once. A bit. But usually others. After my father passed, I worried for my mother. Then I did worry for myself after she died as well."

"How old were you?"

Why do I get the feeling he already knows the answer?

"Twelve with Dad. Fifteen with Mom."

"And you have been on the streets since then?" he presses.

My body shakes involuntarily and I shake my head. "Please … *please* don't ask me about that. If you never ever honor another request of mine, please honor this one."

"Diana. I cannot finish my work with you without knowing what you have been through. And I will do whatever I must to ensure you are fully honest with me." He stands up and plucks the book from the table.

Going to the new cabinet-slash-end table, he puts the book inside and fastens a lock on the doors, placing the key on a chain around his throat, where it hangs next to his silver cross and the key to my ankle chain.

"That is for the attitude you took this morning. I will decide when you may have the cabinet unlocked," he tells me. "And for your reticence, I will return later in the afternoon." With that, he leaves, removing the trash from breakfast as he goes.

The lock clicks, but in my mind I still hear the click of the cabinet lock, and the *other* lock. On my bedroom door. And once more, I have no means of escape, even fictional.

Lying on my side, I close my eyes and let the tears overtake me.

CHAPTER FOURTEEN

Diana

ANOTHER ODD THING I notice, Thomas has never withheld food from me. Being poor growing up, we never had a lot of extra to eat, and then that fat bastard ensured I didn't eat much to keep me skinny and small and young-looking. In stories, people who are kidnapped like this are usually punished by having meals withheld. Not here.

Not that any punishment I have gotten has been nice. But…

No buts, Diana! I scold myself. *Don't start sympathizing with him and this crazy ass place!*

No, it's not sympathizing. It's just curiosity. That's all.

Right?

It keeps my mind busy to think about the mundane things around me. I can't escape, so I can at least stay alert.

Who cooks? The food sometimes tastes different, so do different people cook for the whole cult? I know they have worship on Sundays with the public, but how many people are in this cult, like, living here?

So far, I know of Thomas, Lisa, Catherine, and Father Oliver. Maybe the man who brought the cabinet down too. Were Lisa and Catherine taken like me? "Rescued"? Do men get "rescued" too? What were they like before? What was Thomas like? Was he wild, like the version of him I saw the other night?

If I never comply, will I be stuck down here forever? Or will Thomas kill me like he killed Rick?

The memory of Thomas' sheer energy — never mind the whole rock star look he had going on — makes me shiver. That wasn't a novice pastor. That was a killer. And not a cold one. He killed with passion that emanated from his body in waves. Knowing if I don't comply that he may kill me with that same passion is terrifying.

He'd also fuck *you with that same passion,* the little voice in my head reminds me. *Maybe the first time in your life you actually enjoyed it.*

Shut. Up. I squeeze my eyes shut and tune out my subconscious.

Here's the sad thing.

If he wanted me for me, maybe I'd give in. Hell, I'll join a cult if I am taken care of and cherished.

But I'm not. He wants to save me. To change me. He doesn't care about me, he wants to mold me to some imaginary potential he is obsessed with. No one has ever loved me for me. Not even a crazy man.

I swallow around a lump in my throat.

What am I supposed to do, knowing I will never be perfect for anyone to actually love?

The door to the basement opens, interrupting my pity party for one.

Thomas has something tucked under his arm, and I also see gauze pads and something that looks like an antiseptic.

What the Hell?

"Take your gown off — you may leave your underwear on — and get on your knees, elbows on the mattress as if you are praying. And pray you will, little sinner."

His eyes are hard, emotionless with the exception of the same distaste he had on his face ever since night one, when he pissed on me in the tub. I know better than to try and disobey him. The punishments are violent, but I can handle them. I don't want to provoke him into doing more.

I stand and remove the nightgown; he watches, but dispassionately. No sign of the wild man whom I saw the other night, who would've taken me no matter what.

Folding it, I put it on the bed and then kneel as he told me to.

The faster I do this, the faster it is over with.

"Move your hair so your back is free."

I do so, gathering it on one side over my shoulder.

"Fold your hands before you. You will not move from that position unless I tell you to, understood, sinner?"

"Yes, sir," I reply.

I hear his boots as he walks behind me, at some distance. Maybe two feet? What could he possibly do—

Fuck!

I hear the sound of the whip hitting bare skin before I feel it, and once the sting hits me, I let out an involuntary gasp.

"Good. Let it all out. Cry if you must. Curse. Scream. Unburden your soul so you may be cleansed of the evil within you," Thomas commands. He whips me again, in a different spot, and I bite my tongue.

I won't cry. I had all the tears from pain beaten out of me long ago. If Thomas wants to break me, this isn't how he'll do it. I won't let him.

And that is exactly what it seems like he wants to do as he whips me harder, lashing and lacerating my skin. Hot blood trickles down my back, tickling me. It's an odd sensation in sharp contrast to the pain, and I hate it.

But I won't let him know.

He grunts as he whips me, as if he's using all his force. However, I fear this isn't close to the real strength he has, which would likely kill me. Should I be happy or sad he's holding back?

"Pray, sinner," he tells me. "Pray the pain reaches through your sullied soul."

And I do, unsure if anyone hears me. I pray for relief, for peace, to be loved and cared for and comforted for once in my life.

What did I do that was so evil it required me to live a life of pain?

That thought, asked to a God I am not sure I believe in, almost makes me cry and break. Almost. I won't. I won't let another man shatter me.

The strength it takes to hold myself still, to keep my tears at bay, to weather the pain as if it doesn't feel like my skin has been sliced off, causes sweat to break out on my body. The salt burns the wounds, making my suffering even greater.

If Thomas knew, he would probably be happy.

I refuse to give him that satisfaction.

I lose track of time for how long the torture continues. It could be five minutes or an hour. Tuning it out, diving within myself, helps dull the pain, helps me not react. Only when it has stopped for a few minutes and I hear footsteps do I exit my inner reverie.

Thomas steps behind me and traces his finger down my back, between the open lacerations. I close my eyes, shuddering. He's too gentle. It doesn't make sense. And yet, his soft touch combined with the pain is a heady mix. I could get used to this, and that terrifies me.

"Stay still," he commands, and I hear a hint of frustration in his voice. Something cold touches my back and the sharp scent of rubbing alcohol hits my nose. Only a moment later, my skin is set aflame from the sensation of it hitting the fresh wounds.

If only I could scream, but that will do me no good. It never did. So I dive deeper into myself as he cleans my wounds, wiping blood away, pressing something to them.

Only when the pressure of his hands is gone do I slowly come back to reality and focus on the present.

"You may get up and put your gown back on," he says, the heat of his body gone as he stands up and moves away.

I nod, willing my limbs not to tremble as I stand up and put the gown on, but it's no use. I have no strength left; I used it all up keeping my composure. It's difficult to lower myself to the bed to sit before I collapse. Sweat stings the wounds and runs down my face and I wish he'd leave so I could cry.

Looking up at him, he looks wild once more. His hair has come loose of the half man bun thing he had it in, and he too has a thin sheen of sweat on his skin.

And I can't miss how hard he is; that has to be painful. My blood is on his hands, splattered onto his white t-shirt. Seeing it, combined with his countenance, a wave of lust hits me and I want to die from humiliation.

How could I be turned on at the sight of a man who gets hard after making me bleed?

Thomas stares for a moment before kneeling down in front of me, studying me like he so often does. But the dark heat in his gaze, the barely concealed lust and rage, terrifies me and excites me at the same time.

He brushes his hand across my face, moving the hair stuck to my sweat-soaked skin, and I flinch away from his touch.

Leaning back, he opens his mouth, closes it, and finally says,

"Okay, I need one answer from you now because it's driving me crazy."

Aren't you already crazy?

"What is it?"

"You have dealt with my punishments without complaint, pleas, or flinching. Occasionally, you gasp or whine once, and that is all. Yet the few times I touch you without intent to harm, to punish, you behave as if I am prodding you with a hot poker. *Why*?"

He sounds absolutely exasperated, and that almost makes me smile. Another thing that intrigues me: he has questions about my behavior, just as I do about his.

This time, I can answer him honestly.

"Because ... when you hurt me — punish me — I know what to expect. I'm indifferent to pain; I've been through worse with worse intentions behind the actions. But when you touch my face or my hair, and it doesn't hurt, panic sets in. Because I *don't* know what to expect.

"Pain and I? We are old enemies. I know what pain will do to me, and I am not afraid. Gentle? I don't know what gentleness *is*. I don't know what you're going to do to me, and that terrifies me."

He regards me, taking in what I said. He is so transparent when he's not torturing me; I feel like I can see the cogs of his mind working, decoding what I say and what I don't.

"One day, you will open up to me. But answer me this, at least." He pauses, waiting to see if I will protest, maybe. But I have to hear the question first. I will endure more pain as long as I don't have to relive those three years.

"You can take pain. Have you ever given it?" The darkness I see in his eyes deepens, and a small, evil little part of me likes it.

I think about the principal. How making him bleed gave me a sense of euphoria I haven't felt since. Sticky blood under my nails, on my lips, even in my teeth because I bit so hard. His screams of agony and shock. As my heart begins to race, something in my face must change because Thomas smirks.

"So it seems my little dove has more sin than I thought," he murmurs. He moves a hand as if he is going to touch me and stops.

"I've never killed anyone," I say. *Unlike you.*

"Pity. I should have not sheltered you; I should have brought you with me when I went to visit your former landlord," he muses. "I am sure being chained to me would not have hindered you."

I'm not that girl anymore, I think. *I had the fight beaten out of me long before you ever laid a hand on me.*

"I do wish I knew what you were thinking sometimes." He stands, and I see my blood on his hands, and my heart has not calmed down from the rush of remembering my one taste of revenge.

"No, you don't."

CHAPTER FIFTEEN

Thomas

"UGH, THAT CREEPY dude with the potbelly walked by," Lisa complains as she sits down with her gigantic mug. "I should've poked his eyes out after he looked at my stomach and said what a beautiful daughter I'd have one day."

"I'll kill him for you if you point him out," Hank offers. "Your hands can stay clean. No need to confess any sins."

I smirk. I remember the guy Lisa is talking about; he had an aura about him that screamed malice. I wouldn't leave a plush doll around him, let alone a human being.

"Well, let's hope he walks by again." Lisa smiles. "Now, Thomas asked us here to talk about his fiancée." She nods at me to begin.

"There is something in her past she refuses to speak of, and it's driving me mad," I admit to Lisa and Hank. I needed a breather after the carnage I caused in the basement. The longer I stayed home, I'd recall the smell and viscous feel of her sweet blood, and …

Yeah. I refuse to claim her until she is ready for the ceremony, and she is

not. So I asked Lisa if she wanted to
spend some time on the outside. So far,
Father Oliver hasn't limited any of us
from going out into the world as we
please even when not on a rescue
mission. We just need to ask permission.

"Um … my dude…" Hank hands
me a napkin and points to the side of
my hand.

Glancing at my pinky, it still has
a bit of blood on it. For all it's worth,
someone could think it was paint or
food, but assassins and hitmen know
blood when we see it.

"Thanks." I take it and wipe the
blood away, pocketing the tissue to
dispose of properly. Can't risk it being
found somehow, potentially. I did not

survive this long without using my brain.

"So, what do you think she is hiding? Something like a child?" Lisa asks.

I shake my head. "No. She told me…" I pause to recall the words. "She said pain was an old friend, and nothing I did would break her. But were I to be gentle, she has never known softness."

"You think she wants to trick you into going easy on her?" Hank wonders.

I shake my head. "I know fear when I see it. Apprehension. The silent question of 'what next?' She gets scared when I clean her wounds."

"Then she was abused," Lisa says simply, sipping her latte. We aren't allowed stimulants at the compound; nothing stronger than black tea. She and I get our weekly caffeine fix at this café.

"Her parents passed when she was young. And I cannot find any records of her from the time she was pulled out of private education after her mother passed when she was fifteen," I continue. "Father Oliver and I assumed she was on her own until I rescued her, however…"

"You think she was with someone before you spotted her on that street corner eleven months ago," Lisa finishes for me.

I drain the dregs of my coffee and look up at the sky. "I believe she would stay if given a chance to be a part of the community. I believe she naturally requires care, perhaps not such a heavy hand but guidance. But I cannot fathom claiming her, even if she were to agree, without knowing the truth."

Hank taps me on the head, hard.

"Hey!"

"Tommy, you are hands down one of the most intelligent people I've ever known," he says, "but for fuck's sake, you know nothing about women."

I narrow my eyes at him. "There's a list of former partners who would disagree with you on that."

"He doesn't mean sex, you absolute nitwit," Lisa chides. Of course she'd agree with her friend and not her baby brother. "If a man abused her, she isn't going to tell another man. And she probably won't tell while she's being chained to a bed, even if it is warranted." She lowers her voice as she says that last sentence.

"What do you suggest, O Almighty Genius?" I ask.

She smiles. "Girl's day!"

Diana

I look at Thomas, Lisa, and Catherine as they stand before me. My back itches as the lashes heal and rub against the rough nightgown; I barely slept and had nightmares all night when I did. And to top it off, I'm still mildly horny. So I am certain what I just heard Catherine say has to have been a hallucination brought on by lack of sleep and pain.

"What?"

Thomas gives me that indulgent smile, as if I am a cute cat or something. "You have been with me for one month. One month is the time when habits begin to form, when your brain chemistry changes. While the women believe it is a cause for celebration, I believe it is another test on you." He walks over to me and lifts my left hand up, snapping a metal bracelet on it, too snug for me to slip off. He locks it with his fingerprint.

What the Hell?

"The ladies wish to take you shopping and for coffee and pastries," he explains. "Yes, outside. Yes, I realize you have no clothes; Lisa is going to measure you and bring you something.

"However, everything is a test of both your loyalty and your … tolerance for pain." His hold on me is gentle, as is his tone of voice. His words, however, are mildly terrifying. I've never been loyal to anyone or anything. "This bracelet, the control for which I will give to Catherine, as Lisa would use it a bit too indiscriminately…"

The woman smiles, as if proud of her sadism.

"It will send a selected amount of voltages up your arm if it seems like you will try to escape," Thomas continues. "And the range is long, even if you happen to be a faster runner than either of the ladies. A certain number of shocks like that will stop your heart." He looks me in the eye, and I am too afraid to look away. He's never threatened to kill me before. "Do you understand the consequences?"

I nod. If I want my freedom, I have to be willing to die for it.

"You … you'll let me out even if I choose death over being with you for the rest of my life?"

He nods. "You have to know you wouldn't have survived much longer anyway, little dove. Not the way you were going."

He was right. Hell, there was a good chance a John would've killed me by now already. Especially in that neighborhood. And I can't forget nearly dying on the street after my former "guardian" dumped my body. All this? Ever since I escaped Mike? Borrowed time.

"So, terms are: we go out, we have fun, we come home. You don't run away," Catherine says brightly. "What do you say?"

I look back at Thomas, who is still holding my hand. The gentle touch gives me the creeps. "I talk back at every turn. Why do you think you can trust me?"

"Because I believe, deep down, you trust *me*, and you know you belong here. And besides, I only just found you. I have to pray I won't lose you yet." He steps away and nods at the women. "Sister, Mother. Have a good day."

Lisa reaches into her pocket and pulls out a tape measure. "I think we are almost the same size. Eight?" She moves towards me. "Stand up."

My eyes widen, and she takes it wrong.

"Hey, I can't strangle you with this. Too much give in the elastic."

"No … I *can't* be a size eight, are you kidding? He'll…"

The women glance at each other.

"Thomas was insistent you gain some weight. You were … unhealthy," Catherine explains. "I don't think an eight or a six or even a fourteen would bother him as long as you didn't appear as though you were suffering from famine."

I nod, trying to remember I am not under Mike's thumb. I don't need to look small and young and fragile here. These women certainly don't, though

Catherine is a tiny woman. Her presence, though, is vibrant and not small in the least.

"*Please* stand up so I can be sure and bring you some clothes," Lisa says with a huff.

I nod and stand, letting her measure my waist and inseam.

"You're taller than me, but yeah. An eight. Shoe size?"

"Seven and a half."

She grins. "What colors do you like?"

"I don't have to wear white or pale colors?"

Catherine gives an indulgent smile. "That is a choice, especially when we are at worship or out on rescue missions. Not a rule for all the time."

"I … like black," I admit. "And red."

Lisa returns with an armful of clothes and says, "There's a sports bra; we're definitely not the same size to give you a regular one." She dumps the clothes on the bed next to me and adds, "I'm going to unlock the anklet. The bracelet is on. Consider your movements wisely."

The weight falls off my ankle for the first time in a month, and it hits me: I'm actually stronger than I was when I got here. Healthier. Catherine doesn't look like someone who runs a lot, and I don't think Lisa would want her fake eyelashes to fall off from the exertion.

Thomas is somewhere upstairs, I assume, but probably not guarding the door.

I could run.

I could also die.

Catherine seems like a nice little church lady, but she and her husband condoned Thomas drugging, kidnapping, and torturing me for a month. So I have no doubt she wouldn't hesitate to use the electroshocks on me.

How many times in my life have I wanted to die? Too many to count. Always too much of a pussy to kill myself. So I endured.

I don't have to endure anymore. Not the night terrors, the torture, the solitude. One step out of line and I can hopefully get her to use the shocks enough to stop my heart.

"I only just found you. I have to pray I won't lose you yet."

I shake my head and stand up, wanting to get Thomas' words out of my brain.

I won't tempt fate … yet. Not because of his words; no. Of course not. Because I could have a better opportunity in the future. That's all.

That's all, right?

Lisa brought me the first real clothes I'll ever have worn since I was fifteen. Even during my ten months alone, I mostly wore what I had to in the streets and pajamas at home.

Straight-leg black jeans, black Converse, and a flowy red blouse. Fabric softener, the expensive kind, wafts from them. Luxuries I never dreamed I'd hold. The brands are all designer.

I get dressed and am unsure what to do now when the door opens. Catherine pokes her head in.

"Oh, you look proper lovely!" she gushes. "Are you ready?"

I nod, wondering if this is some sort of hallucination. Thomas used drugs on me once, who's to say he wouldn't do it again?

"After you," Lisa says, gesturing for me to follow Catherine up a sturdy but dark flight of stairs.

I do so, entering a small vestibule with three corridors and one closed door; I assume a broom closet or something. There's white and gray tile, and darker gray paint on the walls with white wainscotting.

Catherine leads me down the shortest corridor, which leads to a living room done in more tasteful gray tones. There is a splash of color in the form of a framed yellow soccer jersey and another splash of pink from flowers in a vase on top of a mantle. Thomas is reading a book on a comfortable-looking light gray couch, and a striped gray tabby sits at his side.

He has a cat?

Lisa goes and hands him the key to my anklet, which he puts around his neck once more before looking at me.

I flinch, knowing whenever Mike scrutinized me, it usually led to some fault and a beating.

He nods. "Enjoy yourselves, ladies. Lisa, you promised to bring pastries back to me. Don't forget." He looks at me again and offers a soft smile before going back to his book.

This is the same man who whipped my skin bloody two days ago? Along with all the other atrocities?

"Come on," Lisa says impatiently. She hands me a pair of sunglasses. "It's been a while, you'll need these."

Designer. My whole outfit cost more than three months of rent at Rick's apartment.

They lead me outside and the warm late spring sun shines on my face for the first time in a month. Catherine stands at my side, I assume to keep me from running before needing to use the electroshocks.

This small, cute house sits on a property near a lake, which has a dock that looks like you can swim off of it. I hear ducks quacking somewhere. There are other houses in the distance, and a small white church with a gigantic white cross.

It's so green. How far out in the suburbs are we?

"It's lovely here, hm?" Catherine says. "When my dear Oliver brought me here, it was just us and two others who wished to build a community." She gestures around. "Look at all God provided."

Did He provide you to Oliver too? I wonder.

"Did…" My throat closes, too afraid to ask.

Catherine turns towards me. "What, dear?"

"Did you and Lisa come here like me?"

Lisa calls, "Not me; my brother and I met Father Oliver and chose to join and surrender our sin voluntarily."

She has a brother?

Catherine looks out over at the small lake. "Oliver saved me from the streets, from drugs. From things the drugs blessedly didn't allow me to remember."

"Come on," Lisa calls once more. "Chitchat while we get out of here for a while."

I get into a different white BMW, not Thomas'. This must be Lisa's, as she's driving. We leave the land — compound? — and as we drive, I see signs of where we are, a small town about an hour or so outside the city.

Somewhere I'd never have been able to afford to live before.

"So, my brother didn't want to tell you," Lisa begins, "but if you stay, and Mother doesn't have to use the shocks on you, he will likely begin letting you out of the basement for a bit."

Wait … Thomas is her *actual* brother?

"You have no real clothes except the nightgowns, so we are gonna go buy you some," she continues, as if she didn't drop a bombshell on me.

"I don't have any money," I say.

Catherine turns to look at me and smiles. "Honey, you're part of the community now, of the church. We all take care of our own. Thomas is making sure you're cared for."

My heart stutters at that, but not in a bad way. Thomas is making sure I am cared for? No one has done that for me. Not since I was twelve.

Lisa parks outside of an outdoor shopping center and we get out of the car. Freedom. All I have to do is find a police officer and—

"Do you think even if I let you out, you'd escape me? The police are in my pocket, you stupid cunt."

If I go to the cops, they'll have to contact next of kin, and Mike is listed as my guardian somewhere, somehow. I may be an adult, but they will still

contact him. He can't know I'm alive, or
he will finish the job.

"Diana." Lisa's sharp voice
shakes me from my reverie. "If this is
too much, we can just walk around or
something."

I shake my head. "No. It's not
that. I'm sorry."

The women exchange glances but
don't say anything as we head into a
store that sells casual designer clothes.

"You'll need some casual clothes,
and a few nicer outfits for church,"
Catherine tells me. "Church is
mandatory twice a week, three times if
we have baptisms. Wednesday nights
and Sunday morning; Saturday
afternoon if we do three days."

I remember going to Saturday evening Mass sometimes with Mom. Dad wasn't Catholic, so he never went with us. That stopped when he died; maybe Mom didn't believe in God anymore.

I wasn't sure I did, either, but someone sent that woman to rescue me after Mike dumped my body in the alley. She didn't find me by accident.

"Can I ask a religious question?" I ask, not realizing I am even going to say that.

"It would be better put to Father Oliver or even to Thomas; he's training under him, you know," Lisa commented.

"But we will do our best to answer," Catherine adds.

"Why would God save a person from a horrible fate just to put them in a worse one, and then a worse one?"

Lisa's shrewd blue eyes see right through me. "Is it really worse, or is it just difficult to face yourself and the sin that seeped into you like a bad smell?"

Don't listen to her, the little voice begs me. *You're still with a man who controls you and hurts you!*

Yeah but … he also sees the good in me. The potential.

I nod and we drop the conversation, both aloud and the one in my head.

Catherine and Lisa are what seems like professional shoppers. They know fashion, and they know just how to dress me to look classy and cute and not overdone. I never really had a style of my own. I was twelve, then Mike had me, then I had to look a specific way for the streets.

"Oh my goodness, wear that the rest of the day!" Catherine says when I exit the dressing room in Calvin Klein with a denim, button-down t-shirt dress.

Lisa glances at my bare legs. "Okay, gotta ask—"

"Laser hair removal. Permanent," I reply, and that is all I will say. I look at Catherine. "I look … okay?"

"Adorable."

"You need a belt!" Lisa declares, and goes to find me one. So far, it seems like her attitude is just … Lisa. Maybe she doesn't dislike me.

Why does her liking you matter? You're gonna escape at the first opportunity, right?

I don't answer my conscience. I can't.

"I've never spent so much money in one day before," I comment, putting my sunglasses back on as we exit the store. I want to ask how the church has this sort of money, since it seems like no one works. Donations? Is it possible? It seems so small, though. Unless the patrons who don't actually belong to the cult are all filthy rich.

"Please. This is a normal Tuesday for me," Lisa comments. "Do you drink coffee?"

I nod. "We aren't allowed it at the um…" I let the question trail off before I call it a cult.

"Compound," Catherine supplies. "And no, no stimulants. But while I don't drink it, you are allowed while you're out. I know Lisa and Thomas escape here for caffeine often." She smiles at Lisa indulgently.

I give Lisa my order and she promises to bring us pastries as well. So she goes inside the café and Catherine and I sit at an outside table. The fresh air feels alien on my skin after all this time.

Closing my eyes, I lean back and breathe deeply.

"God and Thomas really did make an excellent choice with you," Catherine says softly. "I see so much of myself in you. Except … you are much stronger than I ever was."

I glance at her. "How do you mean?"

"I can tell you went through things not of your choosing. Whereas, I chose drugs. I put myself in that situation and Father Oliver still saw fit to save me. You … you had no choice, did you?"

I shake my head, willing the tears not to come. The flashbacks. The fear. Why did Thomas not scare me when he hurt me? When he punished me? Yet a simple memory is enough to send me into a tailspin.

"Can you—"

"Lisa is taking awfully long, isn't she?" I interrupt. I can't go down that road in public. No way.

Catherine sighs and checks her phone. "Oh, actually, she is. Come with me and we can check on her."

I go to say I can wait and watch the bags when I remember I'm not allowed to be alone. For a minute, I forgot I'm still a prisoner. Just one in designer clothes.

We gather the bags and head into the café, which isn't overly crowded.

"There's been a man who keeps acting oddly towards her whenever she and Thomas head into town. I hope he's not bothering her," Catherine says. "Oh dear…"

I look in the direction she is and I've never been more thankful to have only had a banana smoothie for breakfast or else it all would've made a spectacular reappearance at the sight I now witness.

Lisa, carrying a tray of drinks and a bag, stands ramrod straight, trying to avoid eye contact with the man speaking to her. Now, Lisa has struck me as a strong, confident woman who fears nothing. Someone I wish I could be. Right now, she reminds me of a scared deer.

And I don't blame her.

I am an hour outside of the city. Free from the motherfucker for a year already. Yet … he's here. Apparently been here? Still just as fat and disgusting and fake charming as ever, except Lisa isn't buying into Mike's game. She clearly sees he's a creep. If only she knew how much of one.

"No. No, no…"

Catherine turns towards me. "Diana?"

Lisa spots us, relief coming to her face, and as Mike goes to turn and see what she is looking at, I do the only thing my body will let me: I get the fuck

out of there.

CHAPTER SIXTEEN

Diana

I MAY BE stronger but I still haven't run for a long time, and I get out of breath by the time I round the building, so I hunker down, not seeing, not thinking, filled with pure fear.

He thinks I'm dead. What will he do if he finds out I am alive?

"Diana! Diana, please tell me you didn't run away," Lisa calls in exasperation.

"No, she saw something in the café," Catherine says. "That's why I haven't shocked her yet. I don't think it's *us* she wants to evade."

"You better be right," Lisa grumbles. "*Diana!*"

"Don't call my name!" I whine, hopefully loud enough to be heard. "Please, please…" I cover my ears and tuck my head between my knees, wishing I was still in jeans and didn't change into a dress with easy access.

Stupid!

"There you are."

I don't look up, I can't. If he followed…

"Diana, what on Earth?" Lisa whispers. "Why can't we call your name? What happened back there?"

"He can't have seen me," I gasp. "He'll kill me. He'll know I'm alive and he can't have me alive so he'll *kill me*, please—"

Small hands grab my wrists and gently pry my arms from where they are protecting my head and face.

"Hey, nobody is gonna lay a hand on you. Not while we can help it," Lisa promises.

My whole body trembles; I can't stop it. It's nice and warm out but I feel like it's below zero, and I can't focus on anything. Any second now and I will

dissociate and I can't do that when he
might see me.

"We need to get her home,"
Catherine says. "Sweetheart, come on.
Please stand up."

"Can't." I shake my head and
hide again. Just like I used to cower in
bed, in the corner by the wall. Not that it
made any difference. It couldn't save me
then and it won't save me now.

Funny, Thomas said he wanted
to save my soul. As if I can ever escape
my past. As if any pain will remove the
permanent stains on my heart and
mind.

"He might see me. He can't see
me."

"All right, fuck this. Sorry,
Mother."

Did Lisa just curse? My jumbled
brain can't grasp much, until my body
gets jolted. Lisa is strong as she pulls me
to my feet, but I'm unsteady and need to
hide.

"I don't know who you're
worried about, hon, but no one will hurt
you," Catherine assures me. She holds
me on one side, Lisa on the other.
"Come on, let's go home. You need to
rest and you're not going to do it behind
a strip mall."

My breathing hasn't slowed, and
I want to cry but I can't cry. I'm too
scared to cry and blur my eyesight. All I
can do is hide within my mind, sink

back into that place I go when I feel helpless and hopeless, when all I can do is pray to a God I am not sure I believe in that this will all be over soon.

I don't recall the ride back to Thomas' house, only being jolted once more when Lisa and Catherine get me out of the car. Glancing back, I am positive I will see that familiar black Mercedes behind us.

Nothing.

"There's nothing and no one there," Catherine says. "Come on."

Lisa has a key to Thomas' house and she opens the door and calls tentatively, "Tommy? Need a little help."

A deep chuckle comes from down the hall. "How much did you buy that you need—" He rounds the corner, sees me, and stops speaking as his green eyes widen. In a flash he has me in his arms and the strength and warmth should comfort me, but it only unleashes the terror I kept locked away.

"No! Let me go! Let me go, he's gonna find me; *let me go!*" I shriek the last few words and hit at Thomas' arms and chest, but he doesn't budge or let me go.

"Little dove, who? Who's going to find you?" he asks, but I can't speak; I can't say his name or even think about the fate that would await me.

He'd do it all over again, and this time watch and ensure I am dead by the end of it.

"I don't want to give her anything," he says to the women, still trying to hold me captive. I need to run, to get away. Far away. I'm not safe here; not if Mike has shown an interest in Lisa. He may know where she lives. "What happened?"

"Remember that creep who keeps bothering me? He cornered me in the café and when Diana saw him, she lost it," Lisa explains.

"Please let me go!" I shriek, using all my strength to push Thomas away. Just when I think I'm free, his arms come around me from behind, holding me closer, pinning my arms to my sides.

"Shh shh shh," he rasps. "I'm not letting you go, and I am not going to let anyone hurt you. I promise. You're *mine*; no other man is allowed to even *look* at you without my permission."

I start to sob; irrationality and trauma causes me to believe if I stay here, I am going to be found. Taken. Raped and tortured and killed. Why won't they understand I need to leave? Why won't they let me go?

"She's in shock and this is a trauma response," Catherine says.

"She'll wear herself out," Lisa adds.

I sob harder; my throat hurts from screaming. I just need to *go*.

"We can sedate her, but that may make it worse when she wakes up," Catherine says.

I can't get free. I can't escape. So I do the one thing I have not done since that first night when I was thirteen, when Mike forced himself on me.

I beg.

"Don't let him find me! Don't let him take me, please. I don't want to die! I don't want to go through all that again, *please!*" My body sags, my energy flagging even as panic still grips my heart and mind. All I can do is cry.

Pleas are useless. They always have been. I learned that the hard way, that's why I stopped pleading after the first time. No one listens. No one cares.

"Diana," Thomas whispers. He holds me tight; I may be bruised. "*No one* will find you. *No one* will take you away from me. Not now. Not ever." He is all that holds me upright now; I'm too exhausted. "I promise you."

I can't answer, and I think he knows that. I also think he knows I don't believe him.

In an instant, Thomas literally sweeps me off my feet, into his arms, bridal-style. "Open my bedroom door, please."

"Thomas, you know you can't—"

"I wouldn't dare, Mother," he interrupts Catherine. "I am not carrying her down there right now. Let her rest up here."

"I can't rest," I whisper, my voice hoarse.

Thomas walks with me, then I am placed on a butter-soft mattress, my body sinking into it like a cloud. I've never felt anything so blissful. I'm so tired, and my eyes burn from crying, I can't open them much to see the room around me.

When a duvet covers me, I try to kick it away but am too weak to even do that properly.

"Little dove, *stop*."

The sternness in Thomas' voice breaks through the haze and I listen, blinking to clear my eyes of tears. My eyes won't focus.

I want to sleep, but my brain doesn't want to listen to my exhausted body. It still commands me to leave, but I can't. Too weak. Always too weak.

For a moment, I have no idea where I am. It's soft and smells nice, like fancy cologne. Warm. Safe.

I've never been safe.

My eyes struggle to open; they're dry and crusted. My body is heavy; it doesn't want to follow my brain's commands.

My ears work, though.

A soft, deep male voice speaks in a language I can't understand. Fear jolts me and makes me turn my head and force my eyes open.

It's Thomas, knelt at my bedside, his silver cross necklace clasped between his hands; he's praying.

I try to speak, but my throat hurts. My voice manages to make some little squeak, and Thomas looks up sharply, startled.

"You're awake." He drops the cross and it bounces against his chest.

"Here." He reaches for something on the nightstand and in the dim light, I see it's a Powerade bottle. He twists the cap and asks, "Can you sit up?"

I do so with effort, soft pillows making it easier. He hands me the bottle and I take a few sips, my hands shaky as I hold it like a baby drinking from a bottle.

"Do you remember what happened today?" he asks, his voice a low rumble as he takes the bottle from me, putting it back on the nightstand.

I nod, fresh tears swimming in my eyes.

"Little dove…" Green eyes plead with me. I've never seen him look so earnest. His hand twitches. Perhaps he

286

wants to touch me? "I need to know exactly what happened. We cannot move forward… *You* cannot move forward unless you unburden your soul."

"Did you really think what you do to me is the worst I have been through?"

I don't realize I am going to say that until it slips out, and I wish I could take the words back. His punishments are rudimentary compared with my life, but I don't think I'm strong enough to handle them now.

"I did," he replies. "And that was my mistake. But I cannot help you if you do not speak to me. What happened to you, and what does it have to do with the man who always corners my sister?"

"You already judge me based on what you know," I argue. "You only know a fraction of it; what will you do to me when you know it all?"

"Help you heal."

"Torture won't heal me."

He leans back, pensive. "Perhaps not. But I need to hear it from you. I require full disclosure, or else everything I am doing has been for naught."

I still don't speak. I don't know if I can.

With a sigh, he stands up. "I let you out *once* and something happened, and now you won't obey me. How far back are we going to have to go and do this dance again, Diana?"

I shake my head, not wanting to go back to the first few weeks here. I don't think I could handle it again, knowing the cycle will have to repeat.

Just tell him. Tell someone, my conscience whispers. It's self-preservation more than anything.

"If…" I swallow hard and he hands me the sports drink again, eyes still hard. I drink and hand it back to him. "If I tell you, would you punish me for being weak? For not escaping Hell on Earth?"

"I cannot tell you what I will and will not do when I have no idea what you're going to say to me," he says.

I take a breath. "My father died when I was twelve. I found his body."

Thomas nods. Likely, he knew this.

"My mom took a second job to make ends meet, because Dad was up to his eyeballs in debt we had no idea existed. What I didn't know right away was that Mom was being pimped out and testing new street drugs."

Thomas' face is still impassive.

"The man she was working for is Mike Sullivan, he's a businessman on paper but his real money comes from women and drugs … and kids."

"Excuse me?" Thomas' eyes harden again.

"Basically low-key human trafficking. He'll keep a woman and a kid or two to personally rent out, and he sells others. I didn't actually see him do any of that; he just mentioned offhand that he sold some of us off, and the rare few he kept should be grateful." I tighten my hands in the soft, thick duvet. "Mom got progressively more drugged up, lost her first job, and hooking for him was all she had. He pressured her to move in with us, to take care of us. She believed him." I scoff.

How had she been so naive?

"When was this?" Thomas asks.

"When I was thirteen, a year after Dad died."

He nods. "Continue."

"One night I heard him yelling at Mom. She didn't seem to be yelling back; it sounded like she was drugged out of her mind to me. He told her … he said she had one purpose for him and if she was too … can I curse?"

Thomas' lips quirk. "I'll allow it."

"If she was too fucked up to do it, she was warned what would happen."

At my pause, he asks, "What happened?"

"You can't guess?"

"I need to hear it from you, Diana."

I sigh and hide my face, unable to look at him as I admit how weak I was, what I allowed to happen to me. "He came into my room and he… I was *thirteen*! I begged and pleaded and he didn't give a shit!" I didn't think I could cry any more tears, but I was wrong. "I learned quickly begging never does any good.

"And any time my mother was too strung out to service him, he came to me. For the next year and a half, and then…" I hiccup.

"Then?"

"Mom overdosed when I was fifteen. Stopped her heart. It wasn't an accident." My hands clench into fists, closing around the duvet so tight I might tear it. "She was useless to him, too addicted to be pimped out. But that was okay, he could *'get rid of her'*. He had another product."

"You." Thomas' voice is little more than a whisper in the dark.

"He kept me locked up for three years," I continue. "Some of the people who paid to rape me *knew me*. He beat me and raped me too. Withheld food. I needed to stay as small as possible, to look young. All my body hair was permanently removed for that reason, too. And he—"

The sob rips from me as I remember the doctor, and I can't breathe properly.

Thomas kneels back at my bedside, not touching me but his warm hand is close. "Be strong, my dove. You withstood everything I did to you and will do in the future. You can be strong and withstand a memory."

"He didn't want to deal with a baby; it would put me out of work and take too long to sell it — he said he'd *sell it* — so he took me to a doctor and they performed a hysterectomy. He took my mom's happiness. He took her life. He took my childhood. And he took my fucking future!"

I don't care that I cursed two more times than I was allowed, and I'll likely have my tongue burnt with hot sauce again. I can't care. The trauma I repressed since I managed to survive what he thought would kill me is far greater than any momentary burn.

“Diana…”

“I know,” I say through my tears. “I shouldn’t curse.”

“No.” His voice is tentative. “May I touch you?”

He’s … asking?

I shrug. “Does it matter?”

“Yes, it does.”

I nod. Let him get whatever he is going to do to me over with. Maybe I will be lucky and die.

A hand touches my back, and instinctively my whole body stiffens. I don’t push him away, however. Whatever he’s going to do, does it matter? But he doesn't do anything, just keeps a gentle, warm pressure there.

"I wish you had told me sooner," he says. "Can you tell me how you escaped? You said if he found out you were alive, he'd kill you."

Nodding, I say, "He had me gang raped and tortured the night before I turned eighteen. Then had my body dumped, thinking I'd die in the heat… I survived." I did survive. The question is, why? "A good samaritan found me, brought me to a battered women's shelter where a doctor treated me, and that was how I got sent to Rick's building. And I had no job so I … resorted to the only thing I knew."

Thomas exhales, rubbing my back some more. "My brave dove. Look at you, how far you've come."

"What do you mean?" I ask. "I haven't changed. I'm still the same person you brought here and promised to break and mold into whatever perfect Stepford Wife you want me to be."

Thomas arches an eyebrow. "You haven't changed? You truly believe that?" He moves towards me and it takes all my strength not to flinch away anymore.

You know when he wants to hurt you, my mind chastises. *Now is not that time.*

His hand moves hair from my face and he tilts my head to look up at him. "You are a work in progress, yes. But so am I, my dove. You are stronger.

Braver. More beautiful than I could have dreamed."

"I'm still not perfect," I argue. "I never will be. Look at what I've been through."

"Darling girl, who said I wanted perfect?" He grins. "I admit I went about your training wrong. I finally realized that earlier today, as you broke down. As you fought any comfort I attempted to give you until your worn body gave out from the stress. And now … you ensured I knew my methods were incorrect for your unique situation. If I am to slay your demons, I must not feed them." His grip in my hair tightens and his smile widens. "Your eyes dilated. Pain *is* an old friend, isn't it? One you're starting to like."

I don't want to listen, I don't want to believe him, but his words slide into my mind anyway.

"You started to like it once you realized I didn't hurt you for my amusement. I didn't hurt you to keep you in line. I hurt you to free you." He sits close to me on the bed, still holding me by the hair at the nape of my neck. "God brought you to me, and I realize my mistake. You must forgive me, little dove, as I am but human. I was not meant to *save* you. You never needed saving."

He runs his nose alongside my cheek and chuckles when I shiver.

"I was meant to find my darkest hour, my imperfections, reflected in your sin. I was meant to *cleanse* you." He steps back again and kisses my forehead. "I need you to trust me and know this is for your own good. And once I finish cleansing you, we can take the final steps to eternity."

CHAPTER SEVENTEEN

Diana

EVENTUALLY I MUST have fallen back asleep in Thomas' room, but now that I am awake, I see he moved me back down into the basement again, and changed me into a nightgown. I hadn't bought more when I was out, so it looks like the same simple white style.

But there is one difference.

The ankle chain isn't attached.

Before I can even ponder the
implications of this, there is a sharp rap
on the door and it opens. Thomas
enters, carrying a breakfast tray.

"Good morning," he says, and I
return the greeting.

Do I ask about the ankle bracelet
or no?

He sets the tray down and walks
to the cabinet, unlocking my books. "Eat
well and relax today. In the evening,
your cleansing will commence."

"Cleansing?"

He glances at me. "Yes. After all
you disclosed to me yesterday evening,
after seeing your genuine fear, I realized
your soul was not tainted; it was your
body they broke and stained with

wickedness. And I will purge that from within you."

With that, he leaves, and a chill permeates my body.

What the Hell is he going to do to me now?

About two hours after dinner, my door opens again and Thomas enters, carrying a small cloth sack. Metal jingles from inside. He also has a chair he places at the foot of my bed.

I look up from my book, unsure
of what might happen now and afraid
to speak. I was getting used to his
punishments. Now, it's back to square
one.

"Diana, stand up and put your
book down, please," he says. His voice
is softly commanding, not stern but you
know he can be if you give him a
reason.

I do as he asks, more curious than
anything.

"Strip."

A wave of nausea hits me at the
single syllable and I can't believe this,
but I should have expected it. Now that
he knows the truth, he's going to treat

me just like every other man in my life has, except Dad when he was alive.

This isn't the same as when he beat my breasts or ass. There's something different about him now, and I hate this.

"Don't panic," he adds, holding a hand up. "I have no intention of forcing myself on you. When we finally come together as one, I assure you, it will be when you *beg* me for it. Not a moment before."

For some unknown reason, I believe him. My hands go to the hem of my nightgown and I come to find I'm nervous for another reason. A reason previously unknown to me.

I've never been fully naked in front of someone who hadn't paid to hurt me except for him. Someone who claimed to … what did Thomas claim? That he wanted me? Liked me? He never said, just that God chose me for him. Still, this is a brand new situation, and my weight being healthy is also new to me compared to the last time.

"Your eyes speak more than your lips ever have," Thomas comments. "You will not come to harm when you are in my hands, and you have nothing to fear over your body. I find everything about you — from your face to your hair to your body and your soul — undeniably beautiful."

Taking one more breath, I nearly tear the gown off of me, wanting to get this moment over with before I hesitate again. Then the same with my panties.

"Get on the bed, on your back," he then commands.

"Why?" It's out before I can stop it and I know he's getting frustrated.

His lips purse, eyebrows drawn, and if I wasn't in the situation I am, I'd think his pout that is supposed to be angry is actually … cute.

"Little dove, you know better."

I nod. "I do. I'm sorry."

He steps close, arm's length away, and I can barely breathe, but all he does is reach out and brush my jaw with the back of his hand. "You learn quickly. And now that I know your past, your weakness, soon this will no longer be unpleasant for either of us. Now, be good and get on the bed."

Nodding once more, I do as he asks. The sooner this is over with, the better.

As I do, he goes to the cloth sack and removes four sets of manacles. So this was why the anklet was removed. Stupid of me to have assumed it was because I won some modicum of trust.

I close my eyes, willing frustrated tears not to come. I made progress, and thanks to that disgusting bastard, it has all been erased it seems.

Thomas chains my ankles to the foot of the bed first, then comes on either side of me to do the same with my wrists. There's enough give to not cut off circulation, but I can't pull them more than an inch, and that's a stretch.

"Answer me this," he says, walking around the bed while I lay there, naked and restrained, as if this is a normal Sunday afternoon. "You said you begged your stepfather to not rape you that first time. Did you ever fight? Him, or any of the others? Something you said before makes me think you did."

Swallowing hard, I nod. "Once. Only once. The first time he ever pimped me out. It was to my school principal."

Thomas' lips quirk. "Tell me."

I close my eyes, remembering the adrenaline and fear racing through me. The hate. The desire for revenge.

"The first thing I did when he put his disgusting, wrinkled cock in my mouth was bite down. Hard. Blood squirted into my mouth, and he screamed. I kept gnawing at it; when he pulled me off him, the head was partially detached."

I try to stop it, but I smile.

"He hit me, but the adrenaline was still strong. I clawed at him, made him bleed more. Tore away his lower eyelid on one side. Gouged marks in his saggy cheeks. His blood was in my teeth. Under my nails."

My heart races as it always does when I recall this memory. The only good one I've ever had since I was twelve.

"Did you like it?" His voice is low, raspy. Sexy, if this was a different situation.

Oh, who the fuck am I kidding? I'm turned on like crazy right now.

"And if I did?" I challenge.

His grin widens. "Then I know God sent me the perfect bride. Do you know what it feels like to kill the wicked, Diana?"

I shake my head.

"To balance their lives on my bloodied dagger, to hold their fate in the palm of my hand, to listen to them turn from rapists, killers, beasts, into terrified little plebeians begging for a second chance. They never gave their victims a second chance. Yet they dare to ask a messenger of God Himself to spare their worthless lives.

"When I look into their eyes as I land the final blow, it is the most euphoric feeling. The blood that rushes from them, hot and corrosive. The light that leaves their eyes. It's beautiful." His eyes sparkle like gems, and his chest moves as he breathes.

I realize I'm breathing just as hard.

"Do you want to know what that feels like one day? To bring down the wrath of the Lord on the worst of sinners? To the people who hurt you and stained your soul and made me do the things I have to you?"

I nod, afraid to speak.

He caresses my cheek, letting his fingers trail down my neck, stopping before he reaches my chest. "Then be good."

Walking to the foot of the bed, he leans down and this time his smile reminds me of the demon I saw peeking out when he gave me Rick's bloody ID.

And for the first time, he touches me.

A rough finger slides through my wetness, a ghost of a touch, but enough of one to set my nerve endings on fire, and not in a scared way.

I am restrained in a basement
with a crazy future cult leader and I am
more turned on than I ever imagined
someone as damaged as me could be.

What's wrong with me?

His eyes remain on mine as he
looks at his now glistening finger and
puts it in his mouth, sucking my juices
off of his skin. A noise escapes my
throat; one I never heard come from me
before. Of course, it's so quiet down
here, he hears it too.

"You taste so sweet, my scared
dove. And soon you will be all mine.
After I cleanse you from the inside out."

Why has my mind now gone to
the idea he's going to like … powerwash
me?

He reaches into the sack from which he took the restraints and pulls out a black … something. It's small, maybe the length of a video game console but higher. It has an attachment part at the front, and has an electrical power cord. Thomas plugs it in and reaches back into the bag, pondering. Finally he pulls out a cardboard box and removes … a plastic purple penis.

In some of the books I found and quickly discarded, the female leads often used dildos on themselves. Having cocks forced on me and then forcing them on myself, that did not interest me.

He said he wouldn't touch me; he never said *nothing* would touch me.

Oh, please let this be a nightmare, I think as he attaches the dildo to the box.

"I also brought lubricant down with me; it seems I won't be needing it," he comments, sounding smug.

Yeah, I am definitely still turned on. Bastard. Have I always been this sick and twisted, or has he beaten that into me?

"You've had far too many men forced on you. Forced inside you. For six years, if my count is correct." He glances at me and I nod. "This — this cold piece of silicone — will symbolically erase them all. Quite literally rearrange your insides, so that only I will be the one to penetrate you in your new life.

317

"You are unclean, but not by your own doing. Punishment was futile. Cleansing is the only viable option." He presses a button on a remote he produces from the bag and checks that the machine works. He turns it off and moves it, positioning it at my entrance.

I'm not scared. He isn't doing this for his pleasure. But I still don't want that painful, first-thrust feeling. It has always hurt, even when the men were small.

"Look at me, little sinner. Don't close your eyes."

I look up, watching him.

He turns his eyes to mine as he slips the currently still dildo inside me. I wince, but … there's no pain. It's never not hurt before.

You've never been turned on or wet before, idiot, my conscience tells me.

"It's not supposed to hurt, Diana. Unless, of course, you want it to," Thomas informs me with a smile as he sits down, facing me, remote in hand. He sits back, as if he is preparing to watch his favorite TV show, and clicks a button on the remote.

It starts to move, in and out, slowly. Gentler than I ever had anyone inside me before. My panicked heart slows, but it doesn't *still*. No, my body now wants something my brain can't comprehend yet. And my steady, strong heartbeat belies that.

"How does it feel?" Thomas asks after about five minutes.

"Strange," I admit. "Slow."

He makes a noise between a scoff and a chuckle. "*Slow*? My dear girl..." He shakes his head and mutters, "I suppose I have to give her what she wants," before pressing the button on the remote again, and the dildo speeds up.

Not bruising fast, but faster than it was, and a little uncomfortable, so I decide to risk it and move a little.

Big mistake.

I have absolutely no idea what the Hell it is touching, but every single nerve ending in my body is vibrating like they're ready to take flight. A random noise escapes my lips and Thomas laughs out loud.

"I'm sorry; all those men, by choice or not, not a single one ever hit your pleasure center, I see," he says.

That's what this is? Now I understand why girls in books and movies talk about sex so much, if it's supposed to feel like this.

"I wonder…"

He trails off and hits what looks like a different button and my eyes roll back in my head as the thrusting of the machine goes deeper, just a little harder.

Unable to control my body — unsure if I even want to — I cry out as what I realize is my first orgasm ever hits me. Stars form behind my eyes, constellations unlike anything in the sky. My body shakes and spasms, then the machine slows, but doesn't stop.

"Good girl," Thomas practically coos. "How did that feel?"

I don't know how to answer.

"Seems to me you enjoyed it," he continues. "I'm unsure of how much biology you know, but it is a common fact that women can be made to orgasm near countless times in a short span. I believe the last time I ever tested that theory, she passed out around number eleven."

Something in my gut twists when he mentions a past lover. Was she like me? Did she fail and die? Or was she from before he came to the community?

Oh my Lord, why do I even care?

"The more you cum on something without a soul, without intent, the more you will be cleansed," he explains. "You will break tonight, and it will be glorious."

If this is how one orgasm makes me feel, this time, I believe him. His goal since he saw me was to break me.

Now he knows how.

He can't break me with pain, but with pleasure.

Remote clicks, the dildo moves faster than it did before, deeper. I try to adjust, to not make it hit that spot again, but … I want it to.

For the first time, I want that feeling, that brief, euphoric respite.

"Don't move from that position," Thomas commands. "I prefer to wait until after the marriage is consummated to teach you how good it feels to be flogged while penetrated, but do not tempt me."

I would have expected it would take me longer to cum again, but it happens quickly, and I can't stop myself from moaning. After years of fake ones, I am almost embarrassed at how needy and high-pitched I sound.

Thomas watches me, unblinking, as he clicks the remote again, and the dildo keeps plunging but also begins to vibrate.

On the heels of my second orgasm, a third comes without notice and my cries are more ragged now. I grip the thin sheet under me in my hands hard. He said his ex had eleven? I won't handle any more than this; he has to realize that.

"Good girl." He stands and removes the dildo with a slick, wet pop that sounds obscene even to me. He's careful not to touch me.

I sag in relief, letting the sheet go.

"You're still a bit too relaxed, considering I am not nearly done with you," he says, and my closed eyes fly open. His face is expressionless as he goes to the bag and gets out another dildo, this one pink, with something weird attached to it.

"I have to touch you a bit to settle this. Hold still."

The fact he's warning me…

How can he be crazy and kind?

He winds up barely brushing against what a book told me is called the "clit" (sounds like shorthand for a college class; "what grade did you get in clit?") with his thumb and my body feels like it's singing with that slight touch.

But his hand is gone, replaced by the little thing attached to the dildo. It presses right against my clit and the pressure feels like something is sitting in my lower stomach. I can't explain it, but I like it.

"The fact you haven't yet been properly pleasured… When we are wed, you will understand why people claim they see God when they orgasm," Thomas promises.

He sits back down and clicks two buttons. The dildo begins to vibrate and somehow pulse at the same time. It's nestled against that spot that made me see stars inside, but it's the piece on my clit that sends me immediately into orbit as a fourth orgasm hits me.

Another click, and now the dildo thrusts as I still spasm, sending another orgasm floating through me. Wetness spills out of me, slicking my thighs and soaking the sheet under me.

Did … I pee? It doesn't feel like that but… Hell, my mind can barely think a coherent thought. I'm dizzy, heady with endorphins. And now it's beginning to hurt. I've had a lot of men in me, more than ten in a day, but I never exerted myself like this.

Thomas changes the pulsations and I whine.

"Something the matter, little sinner?" he asks.

I manage to look at him again, sitting there with a clear bulge in his pants, once again with a look on his face like he's a lion and I'm a bleeding gazelle. This man would and will devour me if I let him.

"Too much," I whine.

"Oh, no, my dear fiancée. It's not too much yet."

He increases the speed of the pulses and I can't keep quiet as the time passes. I can't count how long it is, or how many orgasms are forced out of my spent body.

I was silent for various beatings and whippings. But this? It's *too much*. Didn't health class once say certain emotions get unleashed during post-orgasm?

I feel it. I feel everything, each time Thomas forces me to come. Everything I repressed, everything I endured, every unspoken prayer and every wish for death. They all come bursting out of me alongside my orgasms and I can't handle it all.

This unleashed all my demons at once, every hidden emotion, and I can't take it as I cry and scream and curse. Especially my fear. My fear that Mike will find me again. That even Thomas and this whole cult can't protect me.

It all flows out of me until I am incoherent, desperate, an utter, true, broken mess on the mattress.

He did it.

Thomas promised me he'd break me, and I think he finally did.

CHAPTER EIGHTEEN

Diana

IT'S WARM, NICE and warm. My body feels limp and loose, as if every muscle has been released from the constant tension for the past seven years since Dad died.

I open my eyes and realize I'm in the bathtub; my favorite lavender bubble bath has been poured in, and the water soothes my aching muscles. I still feel weak and weepy, however.

"You're awake," Thomas says from where he's sat, perched on the closed toilet seat. "Your bed has been changed. As soon as you want to get out of here, I will help you."

I just shake my head; I don't know if I can speak. I feel … I don't know. Empty. Full. Weak. Powerful. Broken. Whole, for the first time.

"Diana, I need you to listen to me," he says, his voice low and grave.

I turn to face him.

"The pain of the forced orgasms, the hormones released, the repressed emotions you brought forth … it was a lot," he says. "And I don't know how much more I can do for you.

"Little dove, you let yourself go this evening. You unleashed everything you could not speak. And in doing so, you were so beautiful. So broken. So fragile. Breaking you was exactly the cathartic experience I'd expected it would be, for both of us."

Cathartic. Is … is that the word I'm looking for?

He brushes wet hair from my face and I don't flinch this time, which makes him smile. "It's been six weeks, little dove. Far, far quicker than Father Oliver told me to expect for the final breaking to happen, for ascension to begin. I think you wanted this, needed it, as much as I did."

I don't answer. Did I want it? Need it?

"I think you wanted all of this, but especially to know you can have a true, pure release, unburdening your soul and your body," he continues. "But I need to hear that from you. I understand you need to sleep on this. Rest. Decipher your emotions. Pray on it should you see fit.

"You have a choice now, Diana. There is little more I can do for you after tonight. The rest is in your hands. I can free you, little dove. But you must willingly give yourself to me first. Let me free you."

"I can't…" My voice is hoarse from screaming, and I clear my throat. "I can't be free while *he* lives."

Thomas' eyes narrow. "Make the proper choice, and you never have to worry about that evil creature again. I promise you this as your husband."

He leans forward and does the last thing I'd expect: he kisses my forehead.

"I will return in the morning. I pray the Lord moves you to make the proper decision."

I wake the next morning with my body still feeling vaguely gelatinous. Very sore on the inside, too. And a small part … wants more. It wasn't just orgasm; it was Thomas controlling it. Controlling me. Sending me over the precipice time and time again until my body and mind felt shattered, yet not letting me die.

Elevating me. Putting my broken pieces together. They don't fit the same, but they do fit. Maybe even better than they did before.

Hell, what am I thinking?

Thomas has:

Kidnapped me.

Drugged me.

Pissed on me.

Cum on me.

Beaten me in multiple ways.

Got hard from said beatings.

Wants me to live on this compound where we need permission to wear dark colors and go into town or have coffee.

Pretty sure he made me think I enjoy pain when I don't (I don't, right?).

Not to forget I still ache inside from that damn machine.

Why am I considering this? Why am I considering his offer?

Because, my conscience whispers, *he saved you from the streets. Sure, he went about it the wrong way.*

He feeds you and ensures you're healthy.

He worries about your soul.

He hasn't forced himself on you, or forced you to be with anyone else.

He killed Rick for you.

He's protected you.

Wait. Wait. Since when did the little voice in my head encourage this? Didn't she always try to stop me from thinking well about Thomas? My own conscience has gone nuts.

"I can free you, little dove. But you must willingly give yourself to me first."

Closing my eyes, I lean back against the flat pillow, hearing Thomas' words over and over again in my mind. If I say yes, if I give in, it's forever. I have to choose now. He has made it clear what he seeks from me. How punishments would be conducted from here on out. How he'd use my pain and turn it to pleasure to the point where it becomes unbearable and I break over and over again.

Or I can remain down here.

Or I can die. Likely, my choice now is between life and death.

And revenge, my conscience reminds me. *You will only be free when you get revenge, and Thomas has offered*

you that on a silver platter. You're a fool not

to take the offer, not to evolve and embrace

what you've always known: you're as evil as

Thomas is, deep down.

Is it evil to kill the wicked? Is murder a sin when you are cleansing the world?

I finally understand how Thomas sees me, sees things in shades of gray. The things he did to me were horrible, but he did them to save me. The things he has done to others he did for the same reason. To cleanse the world. To use the blackness of evil to create the white light of good.

I get it now.

Thomas did break me. He broke the old me, and he's promised to be by my side as I rebuild myself, body and soul.

The door to the basement opens and Thomas enters. I stand up, wanting to speak to him on as equal footing as possible, despite being a good eight inches shorter.

He watches me warily, eyes narrowed, as he puts a cup of tea down. "Did you require something?"

"Yes."

Crossing his arms, he asks, "What is it?"

"You." He doesn't say a word, so I go on, rambling. "I'm sure maybe I'm not perfect for you yet. Maybe you'll

have to work on me in the future. But …
I believe you. I believe I belong with
you. You're the first person who never
harmed me for fun, you've done things
for me others would never have
considered."

Kidnapping, murder, torture.
Yeah, no one would consider those as
acts of love. But he did and still does.
And he did it *for me*. Not for himself. All
he had to gain … was me.

Green eyes soften and he reaches
out, hand brushing against my face.
"You mean it, don't you? You're not
conspiring to escape or placate me."

I shake my head. "I'm not. I …
have been safe here, with someone who
only wants what's best for me. Why

would I ever leave? I don't … I don't

know about love," I admit. "I don't even

know if I am capable of feeling it or

what it is. But I know that when I'm

with you, even if I am hurt, you take

care of me in the end."

"Little dove, love looks different

for us all, and it's all right. God placing

you in my life is enough to prove to me

that love exists, even if you don't know

how to feel it or identify it yet. We have

all the time in the world to figure it

out." He sighs. "I wish you had told me

your truth sooner; perhaps everything

could have been avoided."

"Or…" I trail off, gathering my

thoughts. "Maybe I had to go through

the violence to understand who I am,
really."

That grin. I would wager that
grin terrified many victims and enticed
many lovers in the past. "My work on
you has come leaps and bounds. I'm
proud." His hand moves down to my
throat and the grin widens. "You
understand now the purifying nature of
pain, how receiving can clear your
mind, and delivering it can ignite your
soul."

I nod and he gives my throat a
single squeeze before letting go.

"I will bring you clothes; we have
to see Father Oliver."

He kisses my forehead and then
leaves, and something inside me feels …

different. I can't explain it, but admitting the violence did help me, in more ways than one, feels liberating. I guess the truth really shall set you free.

Thomas returns with clothes and places them on the edge of the bed. "It will be a joy to finally move you upstairs, with me, where you belong. Not that the punishments weren't fun." The grin flashes again. "But now we can be more comfortable should that need ever arise. And for good wives, pleasure always follows punishment. Keep that in mind, little dove."

If I speak, I will likely let out nothing except hot air, so I nod.

"I will wait outside; just open the door when you're ready," he says and exits.

Okay, okay, stop whatever all this is, Diana, I scold myself. *At least pretend to be normal for once.*

He brought me dark wash jeans and a light gray blouse and sneakers, nothing white or extravagant. I dress quickly and make sure my hair is brushed before opening the basement door.

Thomas is scrolling on his phone, and when the door opens he looks up and smiles. "I may be biased, but I do have the most beautiful bride." He pockets his phone and holds his hand out to me.

"We can have phones?" I ask, taking his hand. It's big and warm and rough in mine.

He nods. "We aren't luddites. The reason for this community is because we strive to understand the outside world, not hide from it. It is because we know what goes on out there that we come here, to survive this Godlessness together. We have to be informed. And should things ever get worse, we have a place where doors will be open for all who wish to repent and join us.

"Father Oliver met Catherine when he was just a young pastor, ashamed at the world and his place in it. They started this compound after he brought her to his cabin here to train her and save her. The public attends our services, and precious few wish to go against the grain and join us."

"Or are allowed to be saved, like me," I guess and he smiles.

"Exactly. Now come." He leads me upstairs and I stop once more as we reach the front door.

"No bracelet or anything?"

"No, my dear girl. You said you want to be with me, to surrender your old self entirely. I have to believe you meant it, or else we have no proper start to our lives together," he explains. "I also believe you understand your rather unique position. The same one all who pledge themselves to our community are in, myself included: should you defy us, punishment will be severe … but not swift."

I nod. "I realized the other day my choices were to accept what I am and be with you, or finally die as I wanted most of my life. I chose you. I *choose* you, Thomas."

"That's my girl. Come on. It's not too far to their home, and you can see more of the grounds."

He hands me sunglasses and we exit the house to a perfectly warm breeze. Hand-in-hand, we walk down the clean sidewalks. Each house has its own large, grassy space around it, with many that have gardens.

In the distance, I spot what looks like farmland.

"We keep and slaughter our own animals, as well as garden. We grocery shop for things too difficult to raise or grow, but we try to be sustainable. To not rely on the rest of the wicked world for our needs," he says.

"Except coffee?" I guess and he laughs, really laughs.

"Lisa told you, hm? We all have our vices. Mine happen to be caffeine, blood, and beautiful young ladies whose hands fit perfectly in mine." He winks and we keep walking.

It seems like at least a hundred people must live on this compound, more than I suspected. Children play outside a school, a myriad of ages but not teenagers.

"We don't have a high school," Thomas says. "Father Oliver says the children born here need to experience the real world to understand why they live *here*."

"Do … any of them leave?"

He nods. "A couple have grown and chosen to leave, my first year here. A dear mistake on their part, but it was their right to try."

I don't know why, but I expected Oliver and Catherine to live in a grand home, but their house is as quaint as all the others. The only difference is they and Thomas have the only lake views.

Thomas knocks on the door and the man who opens it is the one who brought my cabinet down to the basement. He has a splatter of blood on his wrist.

"Brother Thomas, are you here for— Oh!" He cuts himself off in shock when he sees me.

"Brother Joseph, meet Diana. My bride." Thomas smiles down at me and I don't know how people greet each other here.

"Nice to meet you," I say, realizing he is looking at me now, unlike before. So he couldn't look at me because I was a prisoner. Interesting.

"Same, same. Thomas bragged about you since the moment he saw you. We're all a bit jealous he met his soulmate, but he's been happier than ever since you arrived," Joseph says. "Anyway, Brother, evidently the other day Sister Lisa cursed and nearly defied Mother Catherine, so she's inside."

Thomas rolls his eyes. "You'd think she hadn't chosen to join the community herself with the way she slips back into her old self. See you on Wednesday."

Joseph waves and I want to ask how community members get punished, but as we walk in, I see I don't need to ask anything.

Lisa hangs from a set of handcuffs dangling from a nail in the wall, her face to the plaster, bare body covered in bloody lashes. Mother Catherine clucks her tongue at Lisa as we walk in. When she sees me, her countenance brightens.

"Oh, Diana! Welcome, welcome!" She gestures to her blood-splattered blouse. "I'd rather not get this on you, dear."

I'm just trying to avoid looking at Lisa.

Catherine can tell and waves her hand in that direction. "Once you choose to be a member of the community, if you don't have a proper partner, punishment is meted out fairly between members," she says. "You'll never have to worry about it, though, dear. Is it too early of me to give my congratulations?"

Thomas shakes his head. "Not at all. We are here to ask for Father Oliver's blessing, as my bride's training has been completed. There was nothing more I could do for her; the choice was hers how she would proceed."

"Wonderful! You will make a beautiful couple, and will surely strengthen the church and community." She turns warm brown eyes to me. "Brother Thomas is in line to follow in my husband's footsteps and lead the community. Being his wife brings a status unlike any other."

I didn't even realize that; Thomas did tell me when we met he was the pastor-in-training.

"Go on and see Ollie," Catherine continues. "I'll finish up with Lisa here."

Thomas nods and leads me down a hall and knocks on a door that reads, "OFFICE". "Father Oliver, may I come in?"

Permission granted and we enter a spacious office decorated with degrees and certificates, as well as framed Bible quotes and a painting of Jesus on the Cross. Oliver sits at a large oak desk, turning to see us.

"Well, Diana, we meet officially at last," he says, standing and holding his hand out.

I take it and shake; he seems much more genial here than he did when he met with all of us sex workers on the street. Not that he ever spoke to me. It was always Thomas.

"Have a seat."

There are two chairs and a leather loveseat, the latter of which Thomas leads me to and we sit down.

"So, I take it you have good news for me, yes?" The light in here is dim, and it seems like he can see me better than he could outside. I've never met an albino person in real life, and I know little about the condition, but I remember reading once they have vision issues.

Thomas seems to be waiting for me to speak, so I do. "Um, yes, sir. Yesterday, Thomas informed me he felt my training and … cleansing was complete or as near as it could be, and he gave me the choice of how I wished to proceed with life." I glance over at him, the soft smile on his face nothing like what I was used to from him. "I chose him. I chose to stay here."

Oliver smiles. "Wonderful! It pleases me greatly. You know, Diana, when someone as high ranking in our church wishes to choose a partner, I have to approve them. And I admit, I worried about you. I see that was needless."

Thomas scoffs, but he still smiles. "You should have worried about *me*, Father. She tried my patience for weeks."

"And she will continue to do so, and you will love her all the more for it, just like my Catherine," Oliver comments. "So, Diana, around here, as it is outside, brides typically prefer to choose their weddings. Some opt for private, just them, me, and witnesses. Some wish for a large gathering at the town hall after a church wedding. The only thing that must be done is the post-wedding consummation before the rest of the clergy."

Nausea roils at the thought of being watched and Thomas catches my hand in his quickly.

"Father … you recall I sent you a message that Diana has had some past trauma. I didn't expand upon it, as it's not my story to tell, but what can be done to not put her through that? To not have a crowd around us?" he asks.

Shaking my head, I say, "Thomas, no, I don't want to cause trouble for you or your traditions. I've suffered through worse."

He pierces me with his eyes. "And that is why I will not let you go through anything to re-traumatize you."

Oliver watches Thomas, not me, with calculating eyes. "You are truly willing to balk tradition to protect her."

"God gave her to me. *I* trained her. *I* saved her. *I* cleansed her. I will not see her revert back to the person she was when she first came to me," he declares.

Oliver stands and paces a moment before stopping and nodding to himself. "The reason for the public consummation is to prove you are joined as one under the name of the First Church of the New Disciples. To shed who you were before. Nothing more than that. I believe I know what you can do to prove that same thing, and not be watched during the process."

He smiles, murder in his nearly

colorless eyes, and suddenly I feel like

everything is about to go horribly

wrong … or horribly right.

CHAPTER NINETEEN

Diana

"YOU'RE SURE ABOUT this?" Thomas whispers.

I nod.

"We can always plan a party for us after, too," he assures me. "Lisa and Mother Catherine will probably beg you to let them, actually. They've become quite fond of you."

Like a pet, I think but don't say.

We walk with Father Oliver to the church, and my legs hurt a bit from the lack of exercise, but I dare not complain. Not now.

Inside, Lisa wears a loose-fitting red dress to not agitate her wounds, and she and Catherine set up bouquets of daffodils and forget-me-knots.

"What did I tell you?" Thomas said to me with a smile. "They must have rushed to our florist for these."

"We did and we are so happy!" Catherine calls to him.

Lisa nods, her eyes tired from her lashing but she manages a smile. "I have a sister-in-law. Funny, I never saw my brother as a settling down type."

"You know God can change a person's very soul," Oliver tells her. "We're still waiting for Him to act on you, though."

Thomas covers up a laugh but it escapes, earning him a death glare from his sister.

She walks up to me and gives me a hug, which shocks me. "I'm sorry I haven't been very nice. I'm working on it, and I'm glad my brother's training worked."

"We will file for a marriage certificate from the government," Oliver tells me. "Sadly, while we would prefer not to, if worse should ever come to the worst, it is best to ensure those heathens cannot question yours or any union within the community."

I nod; I had no idea a marriage certificate was even needed, and I realize there is so much about the world I still don't know.

"Hey." Thomas runs a hand through my hair. "Whatever worried you just now, it's all right. We will work on it all … together."

I nod and smile at him. I believe him.

"If we can proceed?" Oliver asks, gesturing to us to come to the altar. "Have you ever been to church in the outside world, Diana?"

"We were Catholic; I was Confirmed not long before my father passed away," I reply.

He nods. "So you understand the act of Communion; the consumption of the Body and Blood of Christ. We do not do it weekly here. Here, it is symbolic of becoming one in body and soul in marriage."

He produces what I assume is holy water and it's confirmed when Thomas takes it and makes the Sign of the Cross, so I do the same.

Father Oliver then produces the wafer, beginning to speak.

"In Him, two become one. Of one flesh, one spirit, one mind. A bond for eternity no man can put asunder. The

Body and Blood shall bind you both forevermore to each other, and in steadfast service to the First Church of the New Disciples."

He places the wafer in each of our hands and I let it dissolve on my tongue as I was taught to do eleven years ago.

Father Oliver then pours a small measure of wine into a golden goblet, also similar to the one my old church used. But he doesn't stop there. He also produces a small, gold-hilted dagger that appears to match the cup.

"For the life of the flesh is in the blood: and I have given it to you upon the altar to make an atonement for your souls: for it is the blood that maketh an atonement

for the soul," he recites. "Thomas, your hand."

Thomas holds his hand out, palm up, and Father Oliver pricks his fingertip with the blade. Blood wells up, and Oliver turns the finger so the blood drips into the goblet.

Thomas licks his fingertip to stop the bleeding and my mind and body decide to go to war: my body likes the action, my mind is horrified that I'm going to drink literal *blood*.

"Diana?" Father Oliver looks at me expectantly.

"The pain is fine; you'll like it," Thomas promises me, resting a hand on the middle of my back.

I nod and hold my right hand out, and the blade pierces the skin of my index finger. It doesn't hurt much, not even when the blood wells up. Oliver turns my hand over and lets three drops fall into the goblet before releasing me.

Do I just do what Thomas did to clean the blood?

I don't have to ponder, as my very-near-future-husband takes my hand in his and gently kisses the blood away. All of a sudden, I need to remember how to breathe and that my knees are solid, not made of jelly.

Thomas must see the look in my eyes, because he smiles knowingly before dropping my hand. There's a bit of blood on his lower lip and he licks it away.

"The Blood of Christ; the blood of union," Father Oliver says, offering the goblet to Thomas, who takes it and drinks. When he removes it from his lips, they're stained just a bit with red once more.

My turn.

My last chance.

I take the goblet and drink, thankfully not tasting anything except wine, which I realize quickly I do not like.

"*Charity suffereth long, and is kind; charity envieth not; charity vaunteth not itself, is not puffed up. Doth not behave itself unseemly, seeketh not her own, is not*

*easily provoked, thinketh no evil. Rejoiceth
not in iniquity, but rejoiceth in the truth.
Beareth all things, believeth all things,
hopeth all things, endureth all things.
Charity never faileth: but whether there be
prophecies, they shall fail; whether there be
tongues, they shall cease; whether there be
knowledge, it shall vanish away.*

"So says the Lord. We gladly welcome our new member into the community, Diana Hill, heretofore known as Diana Hansen, as she joins with our esteemed Brother Thomas Hansen in holy matrimony.

"The Lord sent our future pastor the perfect bride to mold, to shape, to keep, and to love. Let neither party forget the blessings the Lord has given them; let them forever rejoice in the divine love, hard-won and pure.

"Thomas, do you take Diana to be your spouse, from here to forevermore, including in the arms of the Lord in Heaven? To cherish, protect, and honor; to punish and to reward?"

Thomas looks at me, not Father Oliver, and says, "I do. Forevermore."

"Do you, Diana, take Thomas as your spouse, from here to forevermore, including in the arms of the Lord in Heaven? To cherish, respect, and honor; to walk beside and surrender?"

I wait for panic to hit, to tell me to run, but all I feel … is peace.

This is right.

"I do. Forevermore."

"By the power of our Lord Jesus Christ, I pronounce you wed in the eyes of God, Heaven, and the church. You may claim your first kiss."

And it is my first kiss. No one ever, and I mean *ever*, kissed me. Maybe Thomas knows this, because he is gentle, his beard actually soft against my skin. One hand holds my waist, the other tilts my head just right to reach him.

I could melt right into him and nearly do, my body pressed as close as possible. My mind goes to a movie I watched as a child, *The Princess Diaries*, where the main character spoke of how she wanted her first kiss to be.

This is all of that and more.

I almost wish time could stop and leave us here. Had I known this gentleness awaited me, I'd have weathered the pain better.

He pulls away and whispers, "You were worth working and fighting for, my dove."

"Thank you for working on me," I reply.

Lisa and Mother Catherine interrupt us to give us warm hugs, while Father Oliver looks on, smiling.

When Lisa lets her brother go, she hugs me, and I am careful of her hidden wounds. As she pulls away, she says, "Now, a little birdie told me you have one final task to join your souls as one and let go of your past."

I nod and she hugs me again.

"Good luck, Sister. I am glad I can help you."

Thomas walks me back to his house. Our house? I guess it is ours.

Before we enter, he sweeps me into his arms and carries me over the threshold before setting me down in the foyer.

"I had to be a little cheesy, forgive me," he says as he locks the door. Turning to me, his eyes glitter in the dim, late afternoon light. It spills in from the window, making his blond curls look like a halo of Heavenly fire.

Before I can think any further, he pins me to the nearest wall, hands on my wrists to keep me there, before he kisses me again, and this is the opposite of gentle, yet not forceful.

His tongue slips between my lips and I whimper, wanting more of this. Of him. Wanting him to erase all the others who ever came before him and be the only one my body knows or welcomes.

He bites down on my bottom lip and the sting makes me involuntarily arch my hips to his. He chuckles, licking the wound before pulling away.

"I had to get that out of my system," he admits. "I may be a man of God, but at the end of the day, I am still flesh and blood."

I can feel it, the heat of his blood, the hardness of flesh, through our clothes. And yet I'm not scared.

"Come on, let's get you sturdier shoes and a jacket. We have to be somewhere by sundown, and it's nearly here."

CHAPTER TWENTY

Diana

THOMAS WANTS TO give me one of his leather jackets, but it's far too big for me, so he settles for a hoodie and I put on a pair of hiking boots I bought the other day in town.

Thomas once again looks like he's ready to take the stage at a local rock concert in his all-black, skin tight ensemble. He sees me watching him and grins. "You had that look in your eyes the last time you saw me like this, little dove. Dare I think you rather like me this way? That the darkness left in me calls to its mate within you?"

All I can do is nod.

The doorbell rings and he cocks his head that way. "Are you ready?"

That's a loaded question. Am I? Can I do this? I wait for anxiety and fear and guilt to grip me, but all I feel is a sense of calm, so I nod again.

"I'm ready."

Lisa stands on the other side of the door. "I made the call. You have to meet with Hank first at the location I just texted you," she says. "Ugh, just talking to that creep makes me feel vile."

"Thank you for helping me," I say. "Helping us."

"No problem. I was in the unique position to do so. God be with you." She waves and walks away, and I take a breath before Thomas leads me to his car.

"It's nice being in here without being drugged." It's out of my mouth before I can stop it, and I want to slap myself.

Thomas doesn't seem to be offended as he backs out of the driveway. "I had faith you would take to the training. Had I only known it would take you divulging your trauma to do it…" He sighs.

We drive into town with his hand in mine over the console of the BMW, bypassing the nice area and going into what would be considered the "wrong side of the tracks" in the novels I like to read.

"I grew up here. Lisa and I," Thomas admits. "She always took care of me the best she could; stealing mostly. Then in high school, she started dating this guy, and he offered us another way to earn money. A lot of money."

"What happened to your parents?" I ask.

"Dead. Our grandparents were destitute and didn't care if we lived or died. A part of me wanted to live just to spite them." His eyes don't hold any animosity, just a hint of nostalgia. "Hank's my sister's age, but he already had his apprenticeship under the organization's last owner. Until Hank got rid of him and took his place. And he ensured we lived a good life. When we decided enough was enough and joined the church, he let us go with a promise that he'd still look out for us, if we did the same for him in case police ever came inquiring about his activities."

I want to ask a dozen questions, but I also don't want to interrupt.

"I always had a code: I never killed people just for the money. I killed the scum of the Earth, the people even

Lucifer doesn't want. I became God's right hand here, meting out justice and salvation at the same time. That's why I felt it was right to eliminate Rick; to destroy someone who forced sin upon my dove."

"And why you feel it is right to do it again," I add.

He nods. "Your soul is still burdened. It is time to unburden it." He parks in an alley behind some derelict office buildings and when he gets out of the car, he flashes his cell phone light twice, as if signaling someone.

Sure enough, a man gets out of a pickup, walking towards us. When he gets under the light, he's so imposing my first instinct is to cling to Thomas.

The man smiles at me, but there is no joy in his eyes. They're as blank as that of the skull tattooed on his neck.

"Tommy."

"Hank." Thomas nods and then gives me a reassuring squeeze. "Diana, this is Hank, my friend and former boss. If there was one person outside of the church I'd trust not only with my life, but with yours, it would be him."

"It's nice to meet you," I say, trying to remember Thomas rescued me from Hell. He wouldn't put me in danger. "Sorry I—"

Hank holds a hand up. "Little girl, I can't imagine what this fuckwit up there put you through. Just a quick check on the dark web and the only reason I didn't go up there and end his miserable life already is because Tommy needs you to do this."

He looks over at Thomas and holds out two leather pouches of some sort. "His and hers daggers. That's a first for me."

Thomas takes them both, checks one, and hands me the other.

It's a no-frills piece of metal with a white handle. I can feel the cool steel under the thin kid leather gloves Thomas gave me. His matches, just a bit bigger to better fit his hand.

"I can keep people out for as long as you need, but the timer on the security feed being blocked will only last an hour," Hank continues. "Get your shit done quickly. I know you like to linger over your kills like a lion, but tonight is not the night for slow torture."

Thomas sarcastically pouts. (How do you pout sarcastically? Good question; if you saw him, you'd understand.) "Fine, spoilsport." He turns to me, his free hand now on my shoulder. "Diana. I need to be sure you're ready for this. All of it."

I take a shuddering breath. "I am. I need this over. I need my old self to die so I can live this new life with you."

"Let's go then." He takes my free hand and Hank leads us to an employee entrance.

"I checked; fucker is alone, thinking he's waiting for Lisa. Once you're done, the cleanup crew goes in and we will have all his shit confiscated too," Hank says as he unlocks the door. "Ladies and pastors first."

I find myself smiling a little. Maybe in this new world, I really don't have to be scared of everyone and their motives.

Thomas goes ahead of me, whispering, "Stay close."

We ascend a rickety wooden staircase to the second floor office. Only one door has light coming from behind the frosted glass window on it, and I know he's behind there. I know I have to face him, really face him. I chose this;

Father Oliver gave me a choice on how to set the rest of my soul free and I agreed.

But even as the blood pulses through my veins with excitement and anticipation, fear lingers too.

You have to be strong, Diana, my conscience whispers. *Remember how sweet the principal's blood tasted, knowing you spilled it.*

"Remember, you're not only avenging yourself," Thomas whispers, interrupting my internal monologue. "You're saving countless other people, too."

"I know. I'm … as excited as I am scared."

"Good. Now, let's finish this." He bangs on the door. "Exterminator! We have an emergency cockroach problem."

"Fucking Hell, you didn't have to give me a damn heart attack," Mike yells from inside.

Nausea rolls in my gut and my throat burns with acid. Lungs don't want to work. But I have to be brave. Strong. I have to get my revenge.

He made me into this. Now he has to die with the consequences.

The door unlocks and seeing him — smelling him — this close up makes me feel sicker than ever, but I fight it back. Still ugly. Still fat. Still a monster wearing human skin.

Not for long.

He sees Thomas first, and Thomas lands the first punch before I can even blink, sending Mike flying back into the office, on his ass. He grapples for his chair, but it rolls away, and he flops to the raggedy wood floor.

Funny. He's rich as Hell selling women and children, yet he lives like a pig.

"What the fuck is this?" he yells, trying to get up.

Do you remember those old toys, Weeble Wobbles? They were like eggs almost and you could hit them as hard as a tiny hand can and they'd never stay down, just roll about on their rotund bottoms.

That's Mike right now.

"Hell called. They want their demon back," Thomas says, stepping aside and shutting the door behind me, leaving me in full view of the man who nearly killed me.

His eyes widen and suddenly he's able to scramble into a half-standing position.

"No. No. You're dead. There's no way you survived—" he stammers, cutting himself off.

"Survived what? The gangrape you got paid to hold, where my seventeen-year-old body was nearly torn apart from the inside on the last day I'd be a minor? Is that what you meant to say, you monster?" I challenge, stepping closer. "You thought you'd dump my body in an alley and let me die there like trash while you lived your life scot-free?"

"You're not real!" he insists, shaking his head. "I took too much… It has to be…"

I step closer, kicking at him so he falls to the floor again while I unsheath the dagger. "I'm real. You know, at first, I wondered why God saw fit to save me, when I'd rather have died. But I understand now. God gave me a way to expel all of that darkness you and all those people raped into me. He sent me to Thomas, he sent me to the one person who would give me the clarity I needed to cleanse the world of vile, evil filth like you."

He tries to backpedal, but he's too slow.

I'd like to say I intend on ending this with one blow to his nonexistent neck, but that's not true. I want this to go slow. Just a little. Enough so I know that he has died screaming and begging for mercy.

He never gave me any.

And he won't be shown any.

My blade slices into his gut, about five inches deep. It's smooth like butter; I barely have to exert much force. The acrid, coppery scent of blood permeates the air, as does urine.

He's pissed himself in fright.

"What's the matter? Isn't this where you liked me? Between your legs? Or was that only when I was a child? Why are you scared now?"

Blood soaks the floor; I'm definitely stepping in it, but it's so much fun to watch the terror in his eyes this close, I don't want to move away.

"Please—" Mike gasps.

That's what I want to hear.

"What was it you told me when I begged you to stop raping me when I was thirteen? Oh yeah, *if you are good and be quiet, it'll all be over soon.*"

He raises his hand, maybe to swipe at me, and I slash with the dagger, hitting his palm, and he screams.

Thomas' heavy boot comes down on the appendage, and I hear the bones break as he digs his heel down. "You will *never* get to touch my wife again, demon."

Oh, that's hot. That's very hot. Being actively protected, something I never thought I deserved since I never had it, it activates something inside me.

I'm not alone anymore.

"You isolated me."

Slash to the stomach.

"You raped me."

Another.

"You let everyone pay to hurt me!"

I kneel down to nearly straddle him, so I can reach higher on his chest, stabbing near his heart.

Blood soaks my hoodie and jeans now. It foams at his mouth, but I'm not quite done.

"Mom just wanted a job! She wanted to take care of me! And you destroyed her! But you couldn't get me. No matter how hard you tried, *you didn't destroy me!*"

Finally, I cut his throat from end to end, the blade going so fast it winds up embedded into the scuffed linoleum floor. The arterial spray hits my face and hair and I wipe it away, staggering backwards as a sob tears from me.

Somehow, I remember to take the dagger with me; I can't leave it here.

But I'm not sad, despite the sobs.

Not even close.

I'm *free*.

Thomas grabs me from behind, steadying me, holding me tightly to him.

"Shh shh shh," he whispers, moving my bloody hair away from my face. "You did so good, my dove. So good." He kisses my temple. "It's over now. You won."

I turn and face him, the blood on my clothes getting onto his, making the leather look slick. "Thank you," I whisper. "Thank you for not giving up on me."

He wipes blood from my face, leans down, and kisses me. I cling to him, needing this closeness. What did I ever do without this my whole life?

His body is hard against mine, and as adrenaline runs through my veins, all I can think about is the final act to perform to leave my old life behind and bind my soul to my new husband's.

To willingly give myself to someone in a way I never did before.

The blade is still in my hands, now heavier than it had been moments ago. The part of the old me that remains whispers, *You could kill him now and run. Be truly free.*

I glance down at it, clutched in my hand between us, and Thomas' eyes follow.

He smirks and takes my wrist in his strong hand, bringing my blade to his throat. He discarded his gloves at some point, so his calloused palm is rough against my skin. "Go on. Do it, Diana. If you really wish to kill me, I won't stop you. If that's the fate God sent you to me to fulfill, you won't hesitate." His hand loosens its grip, and for a moment I picture him bleeding out on the floor, dead by my hand, and I close my eyes to savor that for just a moment before I move.

The knife knicks his skin before I put my hand down and kiss over the wound I made, tasting his blood on my lips.

Thomas groans and wrenches me away from him, kissing me again, practically plundering my mouth with his tongue. It's all I can do to keep up, but I need more.

I need him. I need him in a way I never imagined myself needing or wanting a man. Not after my life.

I unzip his jacket and feel his warm skin through his black t-shirt while he shrugs it off.

"Do we have time—"

"We have as much time as we need," he interrupts, kissing me again before he lifts the blood-soaked hoodie off of me. His hands are warm on my waist under my shirt, and because he touched my clothes and hair, they're sticky with blood and leave trails against my skin.

My shirt follows my hoodie, and the way he looks at me makes me feel like more than an object. He makes me feel desired in a way I never knew was possible.

I've never done this before as I lift his shirt off him; never ever actively participated in sex. Now I need to. I *want* to.

Thomas has a slim but powerful body, his chest and arms full of tightly corded muscle I'd noticed even while he was clothed, a slim waist; there is a bit

of blond hair on his chest and then a
trail leading downwards into his jeans.

My hands leave bloody streaks as
I gingerly touch his warm, almost
golden skin.

He moves them from his body
and cups my chin in his hand. "I need to
hear it from you, little dove. Give
yourself to me."

I meet his green eyes, nearly gray
in this murky light, and say the one
thing I never thought I would in this
situation.

"Please."

As if my single plea unlocked
something within him, he pulls me close
in a searing kiss as he unhooks my new

bra — now ruined with blood — and tosses it away.

He kisses down my throat, my chest, to my breasts, taking one nipple into his mouth. So gentle, despite the fervor of his movements. I close my eyes and savor this feeling before he starts undoing my jeans.

Men had done this to me, but not like this. Not to give me any pleasure. If Thomas keeps this up, I may orgasm just from the stimulation. Is that possible?

"I've waited so long to have you, my little dove. Just like this: desperate, wanton, submissive — and all by your choice to give yourself to me."

Thomas stops and picks me up, stepping over the corpse of my abuser, his boots splashing in the pooled blood, as he sets me on the desk, sending papers and a laptop scattering across the floor somewhere behind me.

"Lift up a bit."

I do and he removes my jeans and underwear, on which I can see a clear wet spot and find myself blushing.

"Look at my little sinner; covered in blood and naked, yet red as a tomato," Thomas teases. "Brace yourself and let me taste how sweet you are."

I do, unable to look away as he kneels before me and parts my legs with his hands, baring me to him. When his tongue touches me I can't hold back a whine. His chuckle sends vibrations through my whole body.

He licks me more, then delves his tongue inside, his nose brushing my clit with every stroke.

I know he didn't give permission, but while I brace myself with one hand, I grip his soft blond curls with the other as he brings me closer and closer to Heaven.

When he moves his lips to suck my clit again, I crash over the edge, bright bursts of starlight behind my eyes as I cry out, the only sound in this deathly still office.

He moves away and kisses me. I taste myself on his lips.

Does he want me to reciprocate? I move to kneel but he doesn't let me.

Eyes dark with desire, he says, "You will only kneel for two people, the Lord and your husband. But not here. I want to take my time while you worship me."

He leans me back, the blood on our bodies beginning to dry while Mike's corpse cools on the floor at our feet. Sightless eyes stare up, and I hope he's watching from Hell. I hope he sees what a real man is and can do to me.

Thomas unbuckles his belt and unzips his jeans, pushing them and what looks like black boxers down enough to free his erection, which is already turning a dark red with blood from arousal.

There's no fear, no worry, no uncertainty. Just a pure desire to have him do as he said: erase all other men so I know only his touch.

"Lay back," he commands. "And just feel what it's supposed to be like when you are truly claimed with the Lord's blessing."

I close my eyes as he rubs the head down my wetness, involuntarily wincing as I feel him at my entrance; part of me still expects it to hurt unpleasantly and I assume that won't change overnight.

The sound I let out when he is fully seated inside of me sounds needy

and wanton even to my ears, and it
makes Thomas chuckle.

"You can take the whore off the
streets, but you can't take away what
makes her a whore for a real man."

He begins to move, his body in a
perfect position to reach deep inside of
me, and I'm not shy, making noises I'd
only faked before. I never knew it could
feel like this; be like this.

Thomas changes position and
lays his body on top of mine, possessing
me from the inside out. His breath is hot
against my cheek as he begins speaking
in tongues; unintelligible to me but
somehow I know it's sacred and holy
and just between us and God.

I'm getting closer and closer, and the closer we both seem to get, the faster he speaks, hands grasping mine over my head, pinning me down.

His voice reaches a deep cadence that sounds like music, hips snapping rhythmically as he claims me as his bride, as part of his church, as part of *him*. Like Eve being born from part of Adam, Thomas makes me of his blood, of his body, of his soul.

That thought sends me over the edge and I scream as an intense orgasm rolls through me, sending tears falling from my eyes.

Thomas kisses the tears away in between his holy proclamations, thrusting through my orgasm and right into another one. My body feels aflame from the inside out and all I can do is feel, exist, as he takes me and finishes deep inside, filling me. Claiming me. Owning me.

His words die down into deep moans that make goosebumps rise on my skin as he comes, and gingerly he raises himself up so he's suspended above me, freeing my hands so I can wrap my arms around his waist.

Deep green eyes stare down, pupils dilated, face flushed and covered in sweat and blood. He's beautiful.

"I told you, Diana, you would beg for me to take you. And now, my sweet dove, you own my soul as much as I own yours. Forever."

THE END

ABOUT THE AUTHOR

S.L. Sinclair is a dark romance and taboo author fascinated with human sexuality, murder, and psychology.

Beyond Her Duties was her first release, which made her an international bestseller. Followed by the surprise smash hit *The Family Firm*, cementing her in the dark and taboo genres of romance.

They're part of the LGBT+ community as bisexual and nonbinary and uses she/they pronouns.

When not writing, she's watching horror movies and has her nose buried in whatever book is closest. Sometimes

she actually goes outside.

You can find them on Facebook,

Twitter, Goodreads, BookBub, and

Instagram.